Damned If You Do

Marie Sexton

Copyright

Original publication date, June 2016, by Samhain Publishing.
2nd edition published by Marie Sexton, 2017

EBook ISBN: 978-0-9961741-7-6
Paperback ISBN: 978-0-9961741-8-3

Praise for

Damned If You Do

"…never let it be said I don't love it when the story takes a bit of a turn and I end up feeling sympathy for the devil. Or, rather, make that when I end up loving the devil a whole lot. Marie Sexton made that happen in Damned If You Do, and she did it in the most fun way possible, with a devil who figures, hey, why bunt when I can go for the grand slam?"
The Novel Approach

"The role reversal and irony of the relationship that evolves between two polar opposites provides a nice twist to the story, which has an enjoyable combination of heat and emotion."
Night Owl Hot Romance

"A quick, fast-paced read, but I was thoroughly entertained from start to finish. Abaddon has a *ahem* wicked sense of humor that had me chuckling a few times"
Kiki's Kinky Picks

"Wow! This was so surprising! It was hysterical – first off. Sure, I've seen bits of humor in Marie's writing in the past –but this was a whole new level of humor. It's funny left and right and very, very clever."
Open Skye Book Reviews

"I had a great deal of fun reading this story, wondering if and how the heroes could stay together outside of Hell, and figuring out how the quirky chapter headings fitted in with the plot. I'd love to learn more about the workings of this world's Heaven as well as its Hell, and I'll certainly be investigating other series by the same author."
The Good, The Bad and The Unread

Dedication

Once upon a time, I worked for a large group of doctors. Not just any doctors, either, but *specialists*. Sometimes it was frustrating as Hell (pun intended), but I met many great friends there, including Thalia. Eventually, Thalia and I both left the office behind and found much more creative and rewarding jobs—me writing romance, and her playing keyboard and singing back-up for Mama Lenny and The Remedy. Thalia was an enormous help to me when it came to keyboards and musical duels, so I'm dedicating this one to her. Thank you, Thalia!

Chapter One
The Devil Went Down to Kentucky

Abaddon knew the memo from Satan was coming. Still, his heart sank a bit when the mail clerk stopped at his cubicle.

"Special notice from the boss himself," Damien said, waving the typed page in front of Abaddon's nose. "Somebody finally noticed you hadn't recruited a soul in months."

Abaddon snatched the memo out of Damien's hand and turned away. Damien was hoping to be promoted from the mailroom to actual soul acquisition soon, so of course he was anxious to see Abaddon fail. He was greedy, conniving, manipulative...

Well, he was a devil, after all. Nobody in Hell was exactly altruistic.

Abaddon waited until Damien moved on to the next cubicle before reading the memo.

> *To: Abaddon #325.63.7924.5*
> *From: Satan, Prince of Darkness, Son of Perdition, Father of Lies, etc.*
> *Re: Failure to meet soul quota*
>
> *It has come to our attention that you have not met your soul quota for the month. This is your third consecutive offense. You are hereby placed on*

formal probation. Failure to meet the quota within the next two weeks will result in demotion and immediate revocation of Earth-traveling privileges.

Also: get a haircut.

Of course it wasn't signed. It'd merely been rubber-stamped by one of Satan's many secretaries.

"It finally came, huh?"

This time when Abaddon looked up, he found Baphomet leaning over his cubicle wall. He breathed a sigh of relief. Baphomet was his only real friend—or as close as one could get in Hell, at any rate. "I have two weeks to make good, or I'll be demoted."

"What are you gonna do?"

Abaddon shrugged, glancing around at the rows and rows of cubicles. They stretched as far as the eye could see. Anybody who lost their soul in a wager or an ill-taken deal with a devil wound up here. There were no computers, but plenty of old-fashioned manual typewriters—always with stuck keys and worn-out ribbons—and a never-ending stream of forms to be filled be out in triplicate and filed away. Soul acquisition came with a mountain of paperwork. And the memos! They never stopped coming, and each one seemed designed to stamp out any bit of pleasure one might find at work. No smoking. No chewing gum. No plants on the desk. No magazine cutouts on the walls. No gossiping. No friendly chatter. No laughing.

Absolutely no fun.

There were no breaks, no vacation days, and no overtime. And no matter what anybody put in the break room refrigerator, it always disappeared by lunchtime.

"How bad can a demotion be?" Abaddon asked. "I mean, at least it'd be a change of scenery, and they save all the nasty stuff for dire sins, right? Murder, rape, child abuse—"

"You won't spend an eternity being drowned in the River Styx—" the thought of drowning always made Abaddon shudder, but Baphomet went on as if he hadn't noticed "—but there are still plenty of things worse than soul acquisition. There's laying asphalt around the Lake of Fire, hauling rocks out of the Great Abyss, poop-scooping for the Hounds of Hell, selling flashlights without batteries in the Outer Darkness. And those are just the jobs in the underworld. There are plenty of places they could send you up top too. Mowing lawns in Louisiana in mid-August, cleaning hotel rooms in Vegas, emptying bedpans in a celebrity rehab facility in Hollywood. There's retail work, fast food franchises, lunchroom duty, janitorial work—"

"Okay, okay!" Abaddon laughed, holding up a hand to staunch the flow of words. He hated soul acquisition even more than he hated paperwork, but he didn't feel like listening to Baphomet nag him for two weeks straight. And revocation of his Earth-traveling privileges would be a bit of a bummer. "I get it. Better to go find a soul than risk demotion."

"With the hole you're in, it'll take more than one."

"If I stick to boring, pedestrian souls, sure. But not if I find one that's extraordinary."

Baphomet shook his head. "You're the lousiest devil I've ever met."

That was true, largely because tricking mortals out of their souls was damned depressing. But a nagging conscience wasn't the type of thing a devil could admit to, so Abaddon just smiled and said, "Hey, some of us prefer quality over quantity." He leaned back in his chair and propped his feet on his desk. As always, his inbox was overflowing. His outbox was eternally empty, no matter how many forms he filed into it. "So where should I start?"

That was the real question. It had to be somewhere people were desperate, but still had faith in a vengeful, Old Testament-style God. The suburbs were out—the few suburbanites who still believed in God tended toward a more liberal dogma, and no matter how bad the middle class thought they had it, they were never willing to risk their souls. And some souls were worth more than others. People already bound for Hell were worthless. It had to be somebody who was more good than bad, and it had to be somebody with fair reason to refuse the deal. Sure, you could trade a few sandwiches for the soul of a homeless man, or save a dying child in exchange for his mother's soul, but those were cheap tricks, even in Satan's book. Better to bank on greed, pride, and gluttony than on selfless love or true down-and-out desperation.

"Professional athletes are always a good bet," Baphomet suggested.

Abaddon shook his head. "They've never been to my taste."

"Are you kidding? They're like barbecue potato chips. So good, you can't eat just one."

"No thanks."

"How about New York?" Baphomet glanced around to make sure nobody was paying attention to them before perching on the edge of Abaddon's desk. It was risky being too friendly. They'd have to feign a tremendous argument later where the managers could easily overhear. Maybe even throw a couple of punches. Otherwise, one of them was bound to get transferred to a cubicle far, far away. "It's Fashion Week. Models are always easy pickings."

"There'll be a hundred devils there already." And models were such a bore, about as satisfying as an unflavored rice cake. "How about D.C.?"

"A politician's soul isn't worth the paperwork that comes with it. Besides, we already own them all."

"All of them?"

"Ninety percent of the lobbyists, plus every congressman, senator, and president since the fifties." Baphomet shrugged. "Except Carter."

"Really?"

"Why do you think he only got one term?"

"Huh." Abaddon scratched his chin, thinking. "Okay, Washington's out. How about Vegas?"

"You hate the desert."

"Dubai?"

"Desert."

Abaddon sighed and let his heels fall to the floor. "Then I guess there's only one place left to go."

"Where's that?"

"The Holy Land."

Baphomet blinked in confusion. "Israel?"

"Not that one."

"Oh. The amusement park. Good thinking."

Now it was Abaddon's turn to be confused. He might have thought Baphomet was pulling his leg, but his fellow devil didn't have much of a sense of humor. "There's a Holy Land amusement park?"

"You bet. Re-enactments of the Sermon on the Mount and crucifixions daily."

"That's insane."

"Actually, I think they take Sundays off."

"Still insane."

"It's in Orlando."

"Of course it is." Abaddon shook his head and pushed to his feet. "I'm not going to Orlando, either."

"Then where are you going?"

"Where money is scarce and faith is abundant." Abaddon clapped his hand on Baphomet's shoulder. "To the Bible Belt, my friend. Where else?"

———◇◇———

Once he'd decided on a place, there wasn't any reason to dally. He waited only for Baphomet to be on his way—they yelled a few obscenities at each other first, just in case—then dove into the abyss that resided between Hell and the mortal plane, drifting toward the southeastern United States.

Mississippi was always good, and Georgia, as were certain parts of the Appalachians. He stretched out with his soul sense, feeling and tasting for a particular flavor. He liked his souls devout. No Unitarians for him. Hardly any flavor there at all. He found Mormons a bit salty, and Catholics too bitter, but Southern Baptists were like butterscotch, Methodists like caramel, and a Pentecostal—oh, those were his favorite—their souls tasted like pink cotton candy, sticky and sugary sweet.

Minors didn't count. Acquisitions had to be of the age of consent in whatever country or state in which they presided. Youth was usually more valuable than maturity, but an imminent death was worth far more than a long-range gamble. The devil who'd landed Fidel Castro back in the fifties thought he'd done well, but six decades later, his credit wasn't so good.

The trick was to find that perfect balance of innocence, naivety, and impending doom. A devout, dying, twenty-year-old who was willing to trade his soul for one last roll in the hay with the girl of his dreams? That was the ultimate score. The grand prize. The devil's Holy Grail, so to speak. One soul like that could get a devil promoted to a corner office. Maybe even a cushy pad in one of Hell's suburbs. Sure, you were guaranteed a neighbor who mowed his lawn at dawn, and the HOA was a bitch, but it was still better than the tenement Abaddon lived in.

Stop dreaming and focus! Meet your quota first, then worry about the suburbs!

He needed somebody innocent. Somebody pure. Somebody special. He reached further with his mental feelers, crawling through trailer parks, office buildings, and penthouse apartments. He crept into the woods, up the hills, and dipped into hollows. And then—

"Holy shit!"

There was a soul, in one of the poorer counties of Kentucky. Not just any soul, either, but one that shone like the sun, calling to him from the Earthly plane like a lighthouse in the dark. A soul so pure, it made Abaddon's mouth water and his pulse race. Oh, this one was young, but legal, sweeter than honey on his tongue.

He stayed hidden in the abyss, but moved his mental view closer for a better look.

It was a young man, alone in the woods with a violin. Just sitting on a stump in a small clearing, playing a concerto to the forest. Maybe twenty-two, wearing jeans and a plain white T-shirt, with a knit scarf looped around his neck. His eyes were closed as his fingers and bow moved on the strings.

All alone, in the woods.

It was almost too perfect to be true.

Abaddon took a breath, gathering himself—

And in the blink of an eye, he leapt from the abyss and manifested in a physical body only a few yards away from the boy. He had several forms to choose between, everything from human to full-blown, nightmare-inspiring demon, but this time, he chose to be seen as nothing more than a man in his early thirties. The horns and tail could always appear later, if he needed them, but he'd found that popping into view with them on was a bit more than most mortals could take.

The musician played on, unaware he was no longer alone. For a moment, Abaddon only listened. It was Mozart's Violin Concerto No. 3, and the boy was clearly talented. His fingers never missed a chord. The music rang strong and true through the forest, as perfect as the sunlight streaming through the trees.

Abaddon looked around, trying to figure out where the boy could have come from. They were several miles from the nearest town. He didn't see a car, but the foliage was thick. It was entirely possible there was a farmhouse or a trailhead only a hundred yards away.

He focused again on the boy, letting his soul sense loose to crawl over him, tasting and testing. His pulse once again quickened. His fingertips tingled. A sudden warmth blossomed in his groin and Abaddon's breath caught in his throat. It was the soul hunger, and it was a rush like no other. Abaddon had never tried drugs—or if he had, he'd forgotten—but he imagined this taut eagerness must be what some addicts felt as they carefully pushed their cocaine into perfect white lines. This wonderful anticipation, so similar to arousal, must be what junkies felt as they lowered their face to the mirror. In all his years of soul acquisition, he couldn't remember a single one that triggered his hunger as much as this one.

He took a single step forward in his eagerness.

The bow screeched harshly across the strings as the boy lowered his instrument. "Who's there?" He didn't look around though. He sat ramrod straight on the stump, his head cocked. The sunlight played over close-cropped, black hair. "Hello?"

"I'm sorry," Abaddon said, his heart pounding. "I didn't mean to disturb you."

The boy turned his way, but his eyes never found focus. "Do I know you?"

"No. I heard you playing."

"Oh." The boy's shoulders lost their rigidity, and he smiled. "Peace and love to you, brother. Are you here for the revival? It won't start for another hour or two."

Understanding dawned. *A revival.* Now that the music had stopped, Abaddon could hear voices calling to each other somewhere past the trees. The sound of hammers on metal echoed through the woods along with the distinct crack of heavy canvas flapping in the breeze. It was one of the many reasons he loved the Bible Belt.

"You're part of the revival?"

"I play in the band."

"Of course. You're very talented."

"Thank you."

"What's your name?"

"Seth. What's yours?"

"It's Abaddon."

The boy laughed. "Sure it is. Did my brother send you?"

Even now that they were talking, the boy never looked right at him. Instead, he seemed to stare at some distant point off to Abaddon's left, and Abaddon felt a surge of inspiration.

"Are you blind?"

"Yes."

"Since birth?"

"No. The Lord saw fit to take my sight three years ago, on the day of my nineteenth birthday."

Abaddon smiled. Oh, how he loved the devout. "And what did you do to deserve that? Masturbation? Fornication?"

"Nothing like that." Seth didn't even bother to blush. "It wasn't punishment."

"Really? I thought blindness was one of His favorite ways to smite the unfaithful or the unworthy."

"Not always."

"A test, then? Like Job?"

"No. Merely another part of my journey in His honor. 'I will bring the blind by a way that they knew not; I will lead them in paths that they have not known: I will make darkness light before them, and crooked things straight. These things will I do unto them, and not forsake them.'"

"God and His riddles. What the hell does that even mean?"

Seth simply smiled again, tilting his head like a playful puppy. "Is your name really Abaddon?"

"It is."

"'And they had a king over them, which is the angel of the bottomless pit, whose name in the Hebrew tongue is Abaddon—'"

"'—but in the Greek tongue, hath the name Apollyon.'"

"So you're the devil?"

He could tell Seth still thought it was nothing more than a joke, but he answered earnestly. "Yes."

"Are you here for my soul?"

Abaddon's heart missed a beat. "I am."

"Ah. Well, I'm afraid it's not for sale. My soul belongs to God."

Abaddon had never met God, but he had a feeling He wouldn't appreciate Seth the way he did. Surely a soul so sweet would be wasted on Heaven. "How about a trade then? There must be something you'd like in exchange."

"Nope. God provides everything I need." Seth stood and tucked his violin under one arm. "I hope you'll excuse me. The Reverend will wonder where I've gone. I need to—"

"How about your sight? Certainly you'd like to see again?"

Seth froze, his smile becoming uncertain. He tugged on the scarf, bringing it higher around his neck, as if it might protect him.

Abaddon squirmed, inching closer in anticipation. "What do you say? Your soul in exchange for your vision?"

Seth's brow wrinkled. "You're very strange, you know. Most people don't tease me about being blind."

"I'm not teasing. It's a legitimate offer."

"You'll fix my eyes in exchange for my mortal soul?"

"Exactly."

Seth shook his head, seeming a bit more sure of himself again. "The Lord will restore my vision in His own time."

"You know that for a fact?"

"I do."

Even Abaddon's devilish senses detected no hint of doubt. This boy was a rare breed—a true believer. No wonder he made Abaddon's blood race. "There must be something you want. Maybe a young lady whose attention you'd like?"

Seth shook his head again. "No."

"Fame? Fortune? Those are all things I can do."

"I'm not interested, but thank you, Mr. Abaddon. I have to go now. Peace and love—"

"How about a wager then?" Abaddon asked, desperate to keep Seth from leaving. "A contest."

Seth turned toward him again, his interest piqued. "What kind of contest?"

Abaddon's eyes fell on the violin. "Music. One song each. Best player wins."

"On the fiddle, you mean?"

"Yes."

Seth was still smiling, still thinking it was in jest. "And if you win, you get my soul?"

It didn't necessarily matter that the boy thought it was all a joke. The rules there were imprecise, and Abaddon's soul hunger made him reckless. Seth's soul was the most tantalizing thing he'd ever tasted. Being this close to him was maddening, like the mirage of water teasing a parched man in the desert. Seth would be worth a hundred supermodels, or a thousand politicians in D.C. He'd be enough to satisfy Abaddon's quota for months. Maybe as much as a year.

Abaddon had to have him, no matter what the cost. "Precisely."

"And what if I win?"

"I'll give you a violin of gold."

"A—a what?" Seth stammered, laughing.

"A golden vio—er, fiddle. Whatever you want to call it. One made of pure gold."

"Are you serious?"

"Of course I'm serious." But his answer only made Seth laugh harder, and Abaddon felt disconcerted for the first time in years. "What's so funny?"

Seth's amusement didn't wane. "Oh-ho, that's a good one!" he choked, still laughing. "A golden fiddle! What good would that be?"

"W-well, I don't know. Isn't that the standard trade in these types of bargains?"

That only made Seth laugh harder and Abaddon stood there, feeling more foolish than he had in ages until Seth's mirth finally subsided.

"Oh man, that's funny," Seth said at last as he fought to catch his breath. He wiped tears from his sightless eyes. "A golden fiddle. What in the world would I do with that?"

"I don't know. You could play it, or—"

"You can't be serious. Do you know anything about stringed instruments?"

"Well, I—"

"A fiddle is a work of art, cut from living wood and carefully molded to allow for the perfect resonance of sound through the chamber. It has to vibrate and echo. A golden fiddle would sound terrible. Not to mention the neck would bend the first time I bore down on it. And what about the strings? Are they gold too? Because they'd break the minute the bow touched them. Unless the bow's gold too. In which case..." He chuckled again, thinking about it, and Abaddon feared he was about to collapse into uncontrolled giggling again. "Oh boy, that'd really be something, wouldn't it?"

Abaddon didn't see anything funny about the situation. In fact, he was a bit annoyed at how easily Seth dismissed the offer. He might have resorted to the horns and tail and maybe even a damn pitchfork, if Seth hadn't been blind. "But—but that's the bargain! That's the standard trade—"

"I think I'll pass, Mr. Abaddon. Thanks anyway. And thanks for the laugh too. I needed that."

He turned to go, and Abaddon scrambled for an answer. He had to think of something! Seth didn't want the instrument. But he wasn't opposed to the contest. That was the key.

"What then?" Abaddon called to Seth's back. "What would you take in wager against your soul?"

Seth turned around, his bottom lip caught between his teeth. Abaddon moved closer as he debated, close enough to catch a whiff of that cotton-candy and honey sweetness that made his legs feel like rubber. He longed to reach out and touch him, if only for a minute.

"It seems to me," Seth said at last, "the only fair exchange would be like for like. One soul for another."

Abaddon balked. In all his years filing paperwork, he'd never once heard of a devil gambling his soul. After all, a devil didn't have a soul to give. "I lost my soul a long time ago. I can't—"

"Come to the revival. That's all I ask. Listen to my brother speak."

Could it really be that easy? "If I win, you forfeit your soul. And if you win, I come to your little pow-wow? That's your proposal?"

"Exactly. 'For I know the plans I have for you, declareth the Lord, plans for welfare and not for evil, to give you a future and a hope. For I have trusted in thy mercy; my heart shall rejoice in thy salvation.'"

Now it was Abaddon's turn to laugh. "You're all over the place now. Those verses aren't even in the same chapter."

Seth only smiled. "Do we have a deal or not?"

"Oh, yes," Abaddon said, rubbing his palms together in anticipation. "We definitely have a deal."

Chapter Two
Trippin' Balls on Jesus

The fiddle duel didn't go as planned. Normally, Abaddon would have produced his own instrument out of thin air. The sight of such power normally caused his victims to falter. But this time, before Abaddon could produce the violin, Seth held his own fiddle and bow out to Abaddon.

"I assume you didn't bring one with you."

"Good guess."

Abaddon took it. The bow trembled in his hand. The boy's energy lingered on the frets and strings, making Abaddon's fingertips tingle. And when he put it to his neck and rested his chin in the cradle, the soul essence hit him hard, driving the wind from his lungs. His knees nearly buckled. He gritted his teeth, biting back a moan. It was the strangest sensation, not quite pleasure and not quite pain, like a claw being drawn seductively down his back.

"Mr. Abaddon?" Seth asked, one hand out as if to offer him support. "Are you all right?"

It took a fair amount of strength to straighten his back and shoulders. "Yes." Technically, he was fine, but his mind boggled at the effect the boy had on him. He was both sickened and intrigued. He hadn't felt true arousal in years—maybe decades—but he still recognized the sudden ache in his balls. It wouldn't take much to send the blood flowing south, and then the revival workers wouldn't be the only ones pitching tents in the backwoods of Kentucky.

Focus!

He closed his eyes and took a few slow, deep breaths, centering himself. Trying to forget about Seth and his damnably perfect soul.

And he played.

Being a devil came with certain benefits. No medical or dental, but all devils were granted the ability to understand nearly any language, and to play just about any musical instrument they might encounter. None of them could rival a true savant for style, but Abaddon felt he performed adequately. Mortals usually tripped over their own nerves when it was their turn to play, and by the time he lowered the bow, Abaddon's confidence had returned.

It lasted only a second or two though. Seth's calm smile was all it took to knock him back a step.

"You play well, Mr. Abaddon."

"Thank you." But he could tell it was only a platitude. Seth was compelled by good manners to compliment him, but the boy didn't look scared in the least as he held out his hands for the violin. Abaddon handed him the instrument, being careful not to touch him as he did.

"And you can cut it out with the 'mister' crap. Abaddon is my first name."

"As you wish."

He wondered if Seth could feel him on the violin the way he'd been able to feel Seth. If he did, it didn't show. Abaddon detected no alarm or discomfort as Seth tucked the instrument under his chin and raised the bow. There was no sign of nerves or unease.

"Shall I play Paganini for you? They say he sold his soul to the devil in exchange for his abilities."

"He did, indeed."

"I've always found his work a bit discordant, to be honest. I prefer a more classical sound myself." And with that, Seth closed his blind eyes and began to play.

Really, it was no contest at all. It was the first section of Tartini's Violin Sonata in G Minor, more commonly known as the Devil's Trill Sonata, and it was the most perfect rendition Abaddon had ever heard. Seth's fingers flew over the frets. His bow danced across the strings. He kept his eyes closed as he played, and the music was nearly alive, the chords poignant and heartbreaking, made magical by Seth's wondrous soul, and Abaddon stood in awe as the notes washed over him, lapping against his supernatural senses like waves against the shore. It left him breathless, feeling as if he was only a few chords away from collapsing into tears.

It also left him with zero doubts as to the winner of his little challenge. Seth's soul had never been in any danger at all.

Seth was too polite to declare his own victory though. It was left to Abaddon. He was torn between bitterness and amazement.

"I think it's safe to say you kicked my musical ass."

Seth laughed. "I would never say such a thing, but God has seen fit to bless me in this regard."

"God wasn't the one playing that fiddle."

"I would argue that He was. He merely used me as His instrument."

"Do you ever take credit for anything yourself?"

"To do so would be vanity in the Lord's eyes. 'Every perfect gift is from above, and cometh down from the Father of lights—'"

"Yeah, yeah. I know how it goes." He shook his head. "You have a bible quote for everything, don't you?"

"The answer to every question can be found in its pages."

Abaddon rolled his eyes. It was good the kid couldn't see the amusement on his face. "If you say so."

"Will you come tonight, as promised?"

"I will." After all, a deal was a deal. He was bound by the laws of his own employment to follow through. And looking at Seth, he felt it hadn't been a total loss. "I look forward to hearing you play again. Maybe something a little more uplifting next time?"

"I'll play something fun, just for you." Seth stepped forward, his right hand held out. "It was nice meeting you, Mr.—I mean, Brother Abaddon."

It took every bit of Abaddon's self-mastery to reach out and shake Seth's hand. And once he did, it took every bit and then some to stay on his feet. Electricity tingled up his arm and down his torso, lighting a fire of longing in his loins. He sucked air through his teeth and thanked God—yes, actually thanked the bastard—for making Seth blind so he couldn't see the effect he had on him. "It was nice meeting you as well," he croaked as Seth dropped his hand. "I'll see you tonight."

"Peace and love to you, brother."

"Hell's bells," Abaddon mumbled, running a shaking hand through his hair. "Whatever you say, kid."

The revival tent wasn't the biggest Abaddon had seen, but it wasn't the smallest either. It was approximately fifty by fifty feet, striped red and white. It sat at the end of a long field with an enormous banner erected over the entrance.

Rainbow Revival Tonight

Featuring Rev. Thaddeus B. Rawlins, Jr.
All Worshippers Welcome!

Nearly two dozen travel trailers formed a semicircle behind the tent, obviously the living quarters of the revivalists. Beyond them, Abaddon spotted several vehicles and two semi trucks sitting silent and empty, ready for the day the entire show packed up and moved on.

Abaddon had been to more revivals than he could count. He'd encountered dozens of religious sects through the years, but none like this one. A lot of other revivalist groups held to a very modest set of rules with regard to appearance. Men had to wear long-sleeve shirts, and women wore somber, ankle-length skirts and never cut their hair. But Seth's group seemed to take the "rainbow" part of their name to heart. The men wore corduroy pants, tie-dyed T-shirts, and horn-rimmed glasses. The girls tended toward dreadlocks and long, flowing, bright-colored clothes. They looked like a group of modern hippies, but unlike most "free love" groups Abaddon knew of, this group was remarkably chaste. Shirts were invariably modest, and every skirt ended below the knee. They were a mixture of opposite extremes—garish, yet conservative; devout, but still trendy.

"What do you know," Abaddon murmured to himself. "Hipster evangelists."

The area around the tent buzzed with activity. Men circled it, checking stakes and ties, securing it against any sudden winds. Women came and went, carrying chairs and giant carafes of water, coffee, and iced tea, getting ready for the evening's performance. Generators began to kick on, filling the tent with light, making it seem like a giant firefly perched among ants. All seemed to be working under the direction of a tall, broad-shouldered black man wearing a purple boubou with elaborate gold stitching. His deep voice boomed over the grounds.

The star of the show, as proclaimed by the banner, was Reverend Thaddeus Rawlins. He was about thirty, dressed much like the other men, except he'd added a corduroy jacket with leather patches on the sleeves. He also wore Birkenstocks with wool socks.

Even their reverend was a hipster.

Abaddon lurked near the periphery of the activity, hidden by the trees, waiting for the entertainment to begin. Nobody noticed him, although the eyes of the tall foreman seemed to circle Abaddon's way far more often than he would have liked.

Seth was nowhere to be seen, but the music started shortly after the first car appeared, obviously cued by some vigilant group member. It was "How Great Thou Art", although with a faster tempo than normal, and the hymn flowed from the tent, almost luminescent to Abaddon's supernatural eyes. It bubbled toward him across the packed dirt of the field and broke like water against his ankles, cold as snowmelt on his unnatural skin. That was Seth's influence, he was sure. The boy's soul called to him, beckoning him nearer, making his mouth water with a hunger that had nothing to do with food. He waited though, watching, counting congregants, not wanting to be too near the front of the congregation or too far back. Finally, he fell in behind a group of nearly twenty new arrivals lined up at the entrance of the tent.

The music continued, alternating classical hymns with modern gospel songs. Abaddon had assumed Seth would be playing the fiddle again, but he was wrong. He heard two guitars, a bass, drums, and a keyboard. Seth was at the latter. Abaddon knew that much without even seeing inside. He could tell by the way the piano notes resonated in his chest, jabbing painfully at the well of power that burned where his soul used to be.

The line to enter the tent moved slowly, partly because some of the Reverend's group members stood inside, greeting the new arrivals, partly because mortals were sheep, always stepping through doorways and then stopping dead in their tracks to look around, without regard for the swarm of people behind them still waiting to enter. Abaddon gritted his teeth, willing them forward. He wanted into that tent.

Someday, he'd learn to be careful what he wished for.

The moment he stepped inside, the big foreman caught his arm. His grip was like a vise. His eyes glowered out of his dark face.

"You must be Abaddon."

Abaddon tried to pull his arm free, but had no luck. It was like arm wrestling a black version of Andre the Giant. He subsided into stillness rather than engage in a battle of wills with the man. "I am."

"Seth asked me to watch for you."

The man waited for a response, staring at Abaddon as if he were a particularly loathsome type of cockroach. "Uh…okay." Abaddon shifted his arm again, subtly vying for freedom. He was once again denied. "Well, I'm here. Can I sit down now, or what?"

The man leaned closer. "I must allow entry because it is the way of our people, but I do not welcome you, Brother Abaddon."

The way of our people? This guy had been drinking way too much Kool-Aid, that was for sure. Abaddon did his best not to laugh. "Duly noted."

"I will not allow you to harm the boy."

"Settle down, Captain Caveman." This time, Abaddon yanked his arm forcefully from the foreman's grip. "I'm just here for the music."

He pushed past the man, glancing around to get his bearings. The tent seemed smaller on the inside, but Abaddon estimated it could hold as many as five hundred worshippers. A stage had been erected at the far end, with a lectern front and center. The band played on the right-hand side. On the left, ten of the reverend's select group lingered at the foot of the stage—five women in flowing, broomstick skirts, and five men in corduroys and ties. Abaddon guessed they were the choir. They welcomed the crowd members with smiles and handshakes. They greeted each other with the Kiss of Peace, a chaste kiss on the lips, although never between sexes. Men kissed men, women kissed women. They didn't cross gender lines. Abaddon had seen it before in other sects and always wondered how many of them found some secret thrill in that quick meeting of lips.

He searched for a place to sit, scanning the close-set rows on the right for an empty seat. It was an old revivalist trick to use chair spacing to give the illusion of a full house, regardless of how many people showed up. When the revival first arrived in town, they'd space the chairs a foot apart, making the aisles nice and wide. Seth's revival group had obviously been in this part of Kentucky for a while, because the chairs were packed in, only a few inches between them to allow for maximum occupancy. Abaddon at last found a chair in the fifth row that afforded him a clear view of Seth.

He'd changed clothes. Instead of a T-shirt, he wore a white dress shirt, buttoned almost all the way to the top. And instead of a knit scarf, he wore one of red silk, tied tight and high around his neck and tucked into his collar.

He stood in the center of an elaborate setup, with keyboards on three sides. The band seemed to rely more on improvisation and ornamentation than on strict melodies, and Seth was clearly the driving force behind the jam, like a director without a baton. He played naturally, shifting from one song easily to another, and the rest of the musicians followed.

He was damnably cute, and Abaddon watched him, wishing foolishly the boy could see. Would he search the crowd, if he could? Would he wait to see if Abaddon was swayed by the good reverend's speech? Would he believe Abaddon's soul had been saved?

Maybe it was better Seth couldn't see after all. But even as he thought it, Seth's sightless eyes seemed to settle on him, and the boy smiled.

Was it possible he was lying about being blind? After all, he'd walked in the woods without any help. But no. Abaddon couldn't imagine the boy lying. He was too devout for that, and Abaddon hadn't detected any dishonesty on Seth's part.

The crowd grew louder, and so did the music. One of the guitar players moved closer to Seth, leaning over the keyboard to speak to him. Seth laughed, his fingers not missing a note, his eyes bright with happiness, and another wave of luminescence washed over Abaddon, sending shivers up his spine. He was glad to be sitting, because the desire that welled up in him would have buckled his knees. He clenched his hands, swallowing against the need Seth's soul stirred in him.

He'd claim that soul for himself if it was the last thing he did. He had no other choice. He didn't think he could stand to walk away now.

The music began to wind down, and the crowd buzzed with excitement. The attendees were a motley mix of black and white, Latino and Asian. They cheered when Reverend Thaddeus's opening act—introduced as Reverend Bob—mounted the stage, a tambourine in his hand.

Abaddon leaned back in his seat and watched the show.

The sermon was short on fire and brimstone and long on a New Testament-style celebration of Christ's love. By the time Reverend Rawlins took the stage, half the crowd was on their feet. There were lots of bible verses, at least half of them taken out of context, but nobody seemed to mind. Fifteen minutes into his performance, the musicians started up again. Not hymns this time, but lively music, giving the congregants a strong beat to clap and stomp to as the Reverend raved and the collection plate began to make its rounds.

"The Lord commands us to love our neighbor!"

"Amen!" his back-up and the choir shouted together, spurring the crowd to echo him.

"To love him as your brother!"

"Hallelujah!"

"The Lord commands you to help the poor! To love your brother as yourself!"

"Praise Jesus!"

"We're told in Mark that there is no commandment greater than this!"

"Amen, brother!"

"Hatred stirreth up strife, but love covereth all sins!"

"Hallelujah!"

"And when I leave this Earthly plane, when I approach those pearly gates, when I face my Lord to account for my sins—"

"Praise Jesus!"

Abaddon had seen a lot of religious fervor over the years. He'd seen bible thumping, faith healing, and serpent handling. He'd seen people writhing on the floor and speaking in tongues. He'd even seen a couple of good ole boys in Mississippi drink strychnine. But he'd never seen anything like Reverend Rawlins's Rainbow Revival. All around him, people wearing Birkenstocks, tie-dye, and corduroys danced and clapped and sang. They laughed and praised. It was like a rave without the drugs. Like some little corner of Woodstock where everybody was trippin' their balls off on Jesus.

The music increased in tempo. The crowd cheered. Reverend Bob ran up and down the aisles, shaking his tambourine, making sure the collection plate never stopped moving. Seth played on, his hands pounding the keyboards, his brow glistening with sweat. And Reverend Rawlins—

Abaddon stopped, staring at the stage.

The Reverend still preached, but what nobody but Abaddon seemed to notice was the way Reverend Rawlins and his small band of followers kept glancing Seth's way. Some looked anxious. Some looked hopeful. Seth was oblivious, lost in his sightless, musical world.

"Maybe the Holy Spirit will visit us here tonight!" the Reverend yelled, his eyes sliding again toward Seth.

"Praise Jesus!" the crowd answered, focused on Reverend Thaddeus, even as the choir turned as one to check the young man playing the keyboards.

What exactly was going on here?

They all seemed to be waiting.

Stalling.

Hoping for something.

All but one.

Off to the side, the black foreman stood with his shoulders back and his hands clasped behind him, calm and solid, unswayed by the spectacle before him.

And he was staring directly at Abaddon.

Chapter Three
An Abundance of Baphomets and Beelzebubs

Whatever the reverend's group was waiting for, it didn't come to pass. Eventually, the fervor crested and broke. The music mellowed. The revival came to an end. Congregants shuffled for their cars, mopping their brows with tissue, smiling and laughing. On the whole, they seemed pleased with the performance.

The Reverend's group was different. Abaddon sensed disappointment from them. They continued to glance Seth's way, although only the guitarist approached. He laid his hand on Seth's shoulder, leaning close to speak, and Seth nodded. Abaddon wished he could hear them, but the noise of the retreating crowd was too loud. The guitarist kissed Seth—not in a romantic way, but a brotherly Kiss of Peace—and left.

Abaddon saw his chance.

Nobody stopped him as he mounted the stage and approached the bank of keyboards. The call of Seth's soul seemed to have abated a bit. His cheeks were paler too. He looked exhausted.

"That was quite a performance," Abaddon said.

Seth turned toward him with a smile. His blind eyes seemed to stare over Abaddon's left shoulder. "You came."

"As promised."

"Did you enjoy the sermon?"

Abaddon decided to dodge the question. "I thought the music was amazing." He leaned over the nearest keyboard, taking in the expansive setup. Seth had a Wurlitzer on his right, a Nord Electro stacked over a Fender Rhodes, front and center, and a Hammond B3 on his left. "How many instruments do you play?"

"All of them."

Abaddon blinked. "All of them? You mean—"

"My favorites are fiddle, piano, and guitar." Seth touched the keys gently, as if reassuring himself they hadn't moved. "I used to play harp too, but I don't enjoy it as much since my father died."

Abaddon pictured Seth as a cherub on a pillow cloud, little angel harp in his perfect hands. It brought a smile to his lips. "Electric guitar is definitely sexier."

"Sexier?" Seth touched the scarf around his neck, looking uncertain. "I suppose that's why I prefer fiddle and keyboard."

Had nobody ever flirted with him before? Abaddon wondered at that, but before he could think of a response, they were interrupted by the big tent foreman.

"Brother Abaddon," he boomed, climbing the steps to the stage. "The revival is over. It is time for you to leave."

"Has anybody ever told you that sound just like James Earl Jones?"

The man didn't even crack a smile. "Go home. Seth needs his rest. The performances are tiring for him."

Seth leaned toward Abaddon, smiling apologetically. "Brother Zed is a bit of a worrywart." Then louder to Zed, "It's okay, Brother Zed. We were only talking."

Zed's scowl grew more profound. "You trust too easily, Seth. Abaddon is not like you. You cannot assume—"

"Yeah, yeah," Abaddon said, holding up a hand to stop the man's words. "I'm a bad influence. Whatever." He turned to Seth, who seemed amused by the entire exchange. "Seth, how about you walk me out?"

"That's a bad idea," Zed said.

"That's a wonderful idea," Seth said, as if Zed hadn't spoken at all. He reached across the keyboard toward Zed, stopping short of laying a hand on his arm. "It'll be fine, Brother Zed. I'll only be a minute and you'll be able to watch me the whole way."

Zed glowered, and Abaddon resisted the urge to stick his tongue out like a five-year-old. Seth felt his way from behind the keyboard, taking Abaddon's arm. Even through his sleeve, the contact was enough to make Abaddon's heart pound. He tried to play it cool though. He smiled at Zed as they walked past him. "Nice robe. Peace and love to you, brother."

Zed scowled. Seth seemed unfazed.

"If you could just guide me through the chairs—"

"Of course."

"I do okay outside, but I always have trouble inside the tent for some reason."

Abaddon felt Zed's eyes on his back as he led Seth down the aisle, like a wedding in reverse. He breathed a sigh of relief when they stepped outside into the cool night air. Crickets chirped around them, audible even over the buzz of the revival's generators. The lights from the tent and the departing cars on the other end of the field drowned out the stars and cast an eerie glow over the remaining congregants who stood in small bunches talking to some of the Reverend's group. Seth let go of his arm. Abaddon's flesh still tingled from the contact.

"Did you enjoy the sermon?"

"You already asked me that."

"You didn't answer. My brother is a wonderful speaker, isn't he?"

"Oh." Seth's sect seemed to call everybody "brother", so Abaddon wasn't sure what to think. "You mean you and Reverend Thaddeus are actually siblings?"

"Yes and no." They strolled slowly through the clumps of people toward the parked cars. Now that they were outside, Seth's steps seemed sure and steady. "I was actually abandoned at the revival as an infant. One of the women heard a baby crying in the night. She went looking and found me under the piano bench. Thaddeus Rawlins Senior was the Reverend back then. His youngest son had died of crib death only a few months earlier, so the Reverend took me in."

"Was he the one who named you Seth?"

"Yes."

"The replacement son, given to Eve after Cain had slain Abel."

Seth ducked his head. "Exactly."

They'd moved past the people into the no-man's land between the revival and the parked cars. Abaddon pinched Seth's sleeve, being careful not to touch Seth's skin, and angled them off toward the edge of the field. He didn't have a car, and Zed was sure to notice unless Abaddon could lose the man's surveillance in the darkness cast by the trees.

"So the elder Reverend raised you as his own?"

"Yes. He was a wonderful man."

"When did he die?"

"When I was sixteen."

"I'm sorry for your loss."

"It's okay. 'I am persuaded that neither death, nor life, nor angels, nor principalities, shall be able to separate us from the love of God.'"

He'd shortened the verse significantly, but it was still obnoxious, and Abaddon found himself laughing. "You're gonna drive me crazy with that shit."

Seth only smiled, and Abaddon wondered that somebody so devout could also be so forgiving. "So your brother took over after your father died?"

"Yes. The group changed a lot after that. But for the better, I think."

"They're unique, I'll give you that. Most of the revival preachers working this region are old-school."

Seth laughed. "Oh, I know. I've visited some of their tents. All they talk about is Hell. 'We're all sinners on the road to damnation, so repent now or know God's wrath.' That kind of thing."

"Exactly."

Seth shook his head, tilting it back as if to take in the stars. "I've only ever known one God, and He's not vengeful. He's charitable and forgiving."

Abaddon had always thought of God more as the absentee CEO of an enormous company, more interested in golfing and perfecting His tan than in the activity of humans, but he didn't argue.

They'd reached the trees, and Abaddon slowed his steps. "They were all watching you tonight."

"Who?"

Abaddon stopped and turned toward Seth, wanting to see his face. They were lost in the shadows now. Abaddon's supernatural power allowed him to see Seth's face clearly in the darkness, but the boy's expression was still difficult to read. "Your group. They kept looking toward you like they thought you might burst into flames."

"Oh." Seth scuffed his toe in the dirt, seemingly uncomfortable for the first time.

"Why were they—?"

"It's nothing." But he once again touched that bit of scarf that peeked through the open collar of his shirt, tugging it up higher on his neck as if he were cold, even though it was a pleasantly warm evening.

Abaddon waited, thinking Seth might elaborate eventually. He didn't though, and when it became clear he didn't intend to respond at all, Abaddon opted for a change of subject. "That guy Zed doesn't like me much."

Seth chuckled. "Zed doesn't like anybody much."

"Except you."

"He seems to think it's his duty to watch over me." Another car engine started, and Seth turned his head toward the sound. "Are you parked near here?"

"I didn't drive, actually. I'm a devil. I come and go as I please."

Seth laughed, still thinking it was a joke.

Abaddon glanced toward the revival. It wasn't hard to find Zed. He stood with his hands on his hips, his boubou ruffling in the light breeze, staring in their direction. "You better get back, before your guardian angel over there sends out the search party. Can you make it back to camp okay?"

"I'll be fine, Brother Abaddon, but thank you for asking."

"Thanks for walking me to my nonexistent car."

"Thank you for keeping your word and coming to the revival."

"Uh..." This was getting ridiculous, but he was strangely reluctant to leave. "Thank you for inviting me."

They both fell silent, staring awkwardly at their feet. Abaddon had no memory of dating, but he figured this was what it felt like at the end of the evening, when you had to decide whether or not to kiss the other person goodnight. The thought of kissing Seth made his blood roar in his ears.

It made a few other things happen too.

Zed's voice boomed across the field. "Seth! Enough talk!"

Seth sighed and gave Abaddon an apologetic smile. "Peace and love to you, brother."

Peace and love were the last things on Abaddon's mind. His thoughts were decidedly more carnal. He cleared his throat. "Goodnight, Seth."

He watched Seth turn and walk slowly back toward the tent, which was now dark. He fought the ridiculous urge to call out. To beg Seth to stay, even if only to stand at the edge of the field together a few minutes longer.

And as if Seth had heard that call, he turned. "We'll be here all week. Maybe you'll decide to come back?"

Abaddon smiled, feeling the brightness of Seth's soul all the way to his feet. "Maybe I will."

<hr />

As much as he longed to stay in Kentucky where he could keep his eye and his soul sense on Seth, there was still a mountain of paperwork to do in Hell. But try as he might, Abaddon couldn't keep his focus on his work. He found his mind drifting over and over again to the bright cotton-candy luminescence of Seth's soul, and to the unhappy look on Seth's face when Abaddon had asked what his group had been waiting for during the revival.

"Where in the world have you been?" Baphomet asked, rushing over to Abaddon's desk. His tie was loose and his glasses askew. He held a stack of papers and reports to his chest like a nerd clutching his calculus book. "Did you find some souls?"

"Oh, I found one all right." Abaddon frowned at the form he'd been trying to fill out with his typewriter. He could never get the blank spots lined up right with the strike of the keys.

"Only one?" Baphomet glanced over his shoulder, making sure nobody was listening. "You have less than two weeks to meet your quota, and you only harvested one soul?"

"Damn it!" He'd been distracted and typed his name in the date field and the date in the name filed. He ripped the sheet out of the roller. "You have any Wite-Out on you?"

"Abaddon!"

"What?"

"Do you want to get demoted?"

"Of course not!"

"Then you need to be out hunting—"

"Look, I found a soul, all right? Not just any soul, either. This one is off the fucking charts. It's—"

Baphomet held up the top bundle of papers off the stack in his arms. "Then why didn't I see it on today's report?"

Abaddon sighed. "Well, I don't actually have it yet."

"What? What in the world were you doing up there then?"

"I'll get it, okay? I'm going back again tonight. And I'm telling you, this is it. I found the mother lode."

Baphomet shook his head. "You should quit searching for *the one*, and just fill the quota. Land a handful of everyday, pedestrian souls, and get back in the black."

The thought of a pedestrian soul had never been less appealing. "No way, man. I can't give up on this one. This is the soul to end all souls. The fucking sweetest, purest thing I've ever felt. He's perfect."

"You're such a sap."

"I'm not being a sap. I'm being realistic. This soul is my ticket. I won't have to harvest again for the rest of the year. I'll get a promotion. I'll be King of the Department.

I'll— I'll—break the record!" He paused, thinking. "Hey, who holds the current soul record anyway?"

"Baphomet."

"You mean you?"

"No, dumbass. The other Baphomet."

Abaddon frowned, thinking. "The guy with the red hair?"

"No, the other one."

"The one with the beard?"

"No, the other other one."

Abaddon scratched his head. "The short guy?"

"No! The other other other one."

"I can't think of any other Baphomets."

Baphomet sighed, looking over his shoulder again to make sure no managers were in sight. He leaned closer. "The one with the great big mole." He touched the side of his nose to clarify.

"Oh! Mole Baphomet! I know who you mean now." He frowned again. "That guy holds the record? Who'd he bag?"

"Tom Brady. 2001. Right before that game against the Jets. That's why Drew Bledsoe got hurt."

"I knew that guy was too good to be true! Five Super Bowls and a supermodel wife to boot."

"Baphomet landed Belichick at the same time, but that dude has the soul of a shriveled prune. It was Brady who sealed the deal." He signaled to the eighteen-inch stack of papers in Abaddon's inbox. "You'd know, if you kept up with the memos."

Abaddon rolled his eyes. "That'll be the day."

"Beelzebub's balls, Abaddon! You never take anything seriously!"

"Beelzebub hates it when you use that curse."

"So what? Beelzebub's a self-righteous twat."

Abaddon blinked, confused. "Wait. Which Beelzebub are we talking about?"

"All of them!" Baphomet perched on the edge of Abaddon's desk, trying to shuffle the papers in his hand into some semblance of order. "You need to start taking this job seriously. You've been slacking off for a decade now, barely making your quotas, always getting the work done late. You have to—"

"I know, I know." It was true Abaddon's heart had never really been in the soul acquisition game. It'd always turned his stomach a bit. Then again, he'd never found a soul like Seth's. "Look, I just need this one, okay? After that, I'll... Well, I'll try to keep up."

"No, you won't. You'll wait until the last minute again, just like you always do." Baphomet pointed his finger at Abaddon's nose. "If you're not careful, you'll be bumped down to directing traffic in the Fields of Asphodel. That's where all the cars that used leaded gasoline went, you know."

Abaddon waved him off, sitting up in his chair to lean closer. "Listen, I'm telling you, this soul is so pure it has to get me tenured, at the very least. I just have to come up with a gamble I can win."

"Yeah, good luck with that." Baphomet glanced down the aisle between the cubicles and jumped to his feet. "You heard me, you miserable swine!" he said to Abaddon, raising his voice so whatever manager he'd spotted was bound to hear him. "I hope a pox eats your innards, you pathetic fool!"

Abaddon didn't bother to play his part in the farce. Once he had Seth's soul, he wouldn't need to worry about managers any longer.

Chapter Four
Cock-Blocked by Darth Vader

Abaddon spent his next few days in the office, catching up on paperwork. Baphomet harangued him constantly, insisting he should be out reaping souls. He had a point, but pedestrian souls had never appealed to Abaddon. And now, having tasted Seth's sweetness, he couldn't stand the thought of settling for less. Besides, once he bagged Seth, he'd be set. Why waste his time on a dozen pro athletes when Seth alone would fill his quota and then some?

To that end, Abaddon attended the revival every single evening.

Revivals had always amused him, and the Rainbow Revival was no exception. Zed scowled at him constantly, and each and every night, the Rainbow Revival members seemed to keep one eye on Seth, and yet nothing ever happened. What in the world were they waiting for? Did Seth occasionally burst into flames, or start speaking in tongues, like some of the more extreme Pentecostals? Maybe he had a history of seizures, or of collapsing into fits of the giggles. Abaddon was intrigued by the possibilities, but the strange behavior of the hipster evangelists remained a mystery.

There was no mystery, though, behind Abaddon's inability to speak with Seth again. Zed watched the boy like a hawk, escorting him to and from his trailer. At the revivals, he stood at the edge of the stage, near the right-hand set of stairs, only a few yards from where Seth played, watching the proceedings like a care-worn shepherd. As soon as the revival ended, he rushed Seth out the back entrance of the enormous tent. Abaddon tried following them, but with most of the revival-goers headed in the opposite direction, Abaddon was like a fish swimming upstream.

He was being cock-blocked by a guy in a boubou. It pissed him off to no end. His only consolation was that Seth was irritated by it as well. Abaddon sensed the boy's impatience whenever Zed approached. He watched from a distance one evening as they argued outside Seth's trailer.

"I'm not a child!" he heard Seth say. "And I don't need a chaperone!"

He couldn't hear Zed's reply, but after another minute of quiet complaints, Seth relented and went inside. Soon, the sound of his violin drifted from the trailer, tiptoeing through the night, caressing Abaddon's senses, teasing him with possibilities. It was as if Seth knew he was there and was playing just for him. Abaddon's mouth watered and his groin tingled as he thought how glorious it would feel to claim Seth's soul for himself. It was almost as if Seth were issuing an invitation, but Zed stood just outside the trailer's door, staring toward the woods where Abaddon hid.

Abaddon debated simply manifesting inside Seth's trailer, but that seemed rude, even by devil standards. Besides, popping into existence was bound to startle Seth, and if he made any noise at all, Zed would come barreling in, bringing the wrath of the entire revival down on Abaddon's head. Local law enforcement might even get involved, and getting arrested was such a hassle. Sure, he could just disappear into the abyss, but then there'd be manhunts and news reports and APBs…

The paperwork alone would take a week, and Seth probably wouldn't give him the time of day afterwards.

No. Better to bide his time.

But after two full hours, Seth's trailer had gone dark and silent, and Zed still stood guard. Abaddon eventually conceded defeat and returned to Hell. After all, paperwork still waited. He was more behind on his work than ever.

On the fifth night of the revival, his luck finally changed.

He arrived at the tent earlier than he had on previous nights. As usual, Zed escorted Seth to the tent. Even somebody without supernatural senses might have picked up on Seth's anger based on the set of his jaw and the darkness in his eyes, but to Abaddon, that suppressed rage was like hickory syrup on Seth's cotton-candy soul. It gave his essence a thick, almost smoky flavor that sent shivers up Abaddon's spine.

No matter where he sat in the congregation, he swore Seth's blind eyes found him every time. Seth smiled in his direction, biting his lip and turning away self-consciously. He'd played guitar the previous two nights, but this time, he returned to his place behind the keyboards. He wore jeans and a plain black T-shirt, with a rainbow scarf around his neck. Abaddon took a seat at the front of the house, directly in front of Seth. Zed glowered at him, and Abaddon raised his hand in a jaunty wave and had to suppress a childish giggle at the stain of fury that climbed Zed's dark cheeks.

The tent filled quickly and the revival kicked into gear. Thaddeus and Reverend Bob worked the crowd. The choir sang praises. Twenty minutes into the revival, Abaddon was the only member of the audience still sitting. The rest danced and waved their hands in the air, shouting "hallelujah!" and "praise Jesus!" on cue. The tent seemed to swell and vibrate with their fervor. So many souls he might claim, but none that called to him as Seth's did.

Seth's playing was perfect, as always. But tonight, Abaddon detected a hollowness to it. Seth wasn't smiling as easily as usual. The chords from his electric keyboard felt flat and lifeless against Abaddon's senses, resounding more with loneliness than with joy.

He was unhappy. That much was clear.

Abaddon smiled. Now, he had something to work with. Seth's resentment of Zed's helicopter parenting was just the spark he'd been waiting for. He needed only to fan it a bit, make an offer that played on Seth's anger and gave it a way to blaze free. He'd let that fury burn over him like a wildfire, and when it was done, Seth would belong to him.

Or so he hoped, at any rate.

An hour later, the tent had devolved into borderline chaos. Congregants danced and sang. The collection plate went past him again and again. Reverend Bob pounded his tambourine and Thaddeus preached, waving his bible in the air. The choir had spread across the stage, waving their arms, singing the most rocking version of "Bosom of Abraham" Abaddon had ever heard.

Abaddon waited, biding his time, hoping that tonight, he'd be close enough to catch Seth before Zed could stop him.

A woman to his left cried out in religious ecstasy, somehow making herself heard over the din. She shook her arms, jerking her body in controlled convulsions, babbling nonsensically in a language that didn't exist. The crowd circled around her, cheering her on, some of them simply enjoying the spectacle, some wanting to be closer to her as she was stirred to passion by God's invisible touch.

Abaddon shook his head in amusement. He'd seen hundreds of people do the "speaking in tongues" routine.

He'd been to revivals where half the attendees collapsed and writhed across the floor like slices of bacon in a pan, but until now, the Rainbow Revival had been low on such theatrics.

"Let's give her some room, now!" Thaddeus cried, holding his arms wide. "The Lord's touch is a powerful thing. Brother Zed, help our devout sister to a chair. She'll need to rest after such divine inspiration."

Zed scowled, but did as instructed, abandoning his post at the foot of the stairs.

Abaddon saw his chance, and he took it.

Nobody even noticed as he left his seat and climbed the flight of steps on the right end of the stage. Nobody gave him a second glance as he squeezed past the choir and made his way to Seth and the keyboards. Seth's fingers were fast on the ivories, but his heart wasn't in it. Abaddon stepped up behind him, so close he could have touched him, savoring the sweetness that lingered in the air. Even tainted with anger and sadness, Seth's soul made his mouth water.

"Not bad, kid. But I think you're holding back."

Seth didn't miss a beat, but his head whipped toward Abaddon, a pleased smile spreading across his face. "I knew you were here."

Abaddon tested the organ on Seth's left, adjusting the volume and drawbars a bit. "Mind if I jump in?"

The glow of Seth's soul seemed to pulse, growing warmer, like the heat from a campfire against Abaddon's skin. He bit his lower lip, glancing sideways at Abaddon without missing a note. "Go right ahead."

It only took Abaddon a minute to get a feel for the song. Seth was keeping the melody simple, allowing Abaddon a chance to figure out the chords. Abaddon nudged him with his elbow. "Is that all you've got?"

Seth laughed. His amusement at being challenged again was the sweetest aphrodisiac Abaddon had ever known. "Are we talking about another contest, old man?"

"'Old man'? What'd I do to deserve that?"

"What are we playing for this time?"

"Your mortal soul."

"And if I win?"

"Name it."

"You owe me ice cream."

"Is that it?"

Seth laughed. "That's it. Now see if you can keep up."

And with that, he left "simple" behind and shifted into a rambunctious rendition of "Lead Me To That Rock", giving it a strong, bluesy, southern kick. His drummer followed easily, but the guitar and bass players both stumbled with the sudden transition. The choir picked it up fast, raising their hands to the sky as they sang out the first verse.

> *From the ends of the Earth*
> *From the ends of the Earth*
> *Will I cry unto thee*

The crowd joined in. The notes from Seth's keyboard took on a new flavor, echoing through Abaddon's soul senses, brightening the entire tent. The congregation felt it, whether they knew it or not. Seth's joy was contagious, and Thaddeus gave up preaching, letting the fervor take hold.

> *Lead me to that rock*
> *Lead me to that rock*
> *That is higher than I*

After that, Seth amped them into "Daddy Sang Bass", losing his guitarist in the process. The young man didn't seem upset, though. He laughed, as if he was used to being smoked by Seth during the heavy improvisation. He traded his guitar for a bottle of water out of a cooler hidden behind the drum set and sat back to watch the show.

The bassist and drummer fared a bit better. The choir followed enthusiastically as Seth transitioned into "Can't Nobody Do Me Like Jesus", the title of which always brought sinful images to Abaddon's mind and made him chuckle. And finally, Seth drove them into a rip-roaring, ragtime rendition of "Jesus, Hold My Hand".

The tent shook. The noise was deafening. Seth laughed at Abaddon constantly, calling key changes to him once or twice when Abaddon missed them, and Abaddon tripped along, his forearms burning, tapping into every ounce of his Hell-given musical talent, but he'd never win. He knew the basics, but he couldn't jam on Seth's level. Seth gave him just enough time after each change to catch onto his rhythm—just enough time to match him—before kicking his own part into heavy ornamentation. Abaddon wasn't competing with Seth. He was playing backup, supplying the rhythm to underscore Seth's true talent, but somehow, it suited him.

The pace was frantic, Seth's smile and laugh truly glorious, and Abaddon found himself laughing too, loving the wonder of the moment, as caught up in the excitement as the congregants, but his infatuation had nothing to do with God and salvation and everything to do with the angelic muse at his side. It was the most fun he'd had in years.

Zed stood at the foot of the stage like some biblical pillar of rage and Abaddon found himself laughing more, hoping the moment went on forever.

It didn't though.

"Last time!" Seth called over his shoulder toward the choir and the drummer.

They shifted keys, driving toward the finale, building to a crescendo, and when it finally ended, the crowd cheered. The choir collapsed to their seats, fanning themselves and wiping sweat from their brows. Thaddeus stepped forward again, his arms in the air as he prepared to give the final segment of his sermon.

And Seth...

Seth turned to Abaddon and threw his arms around his neck, laughing in delight. "That was amazing!"

All of Seth's energy slammed into Abaddon like a fist in the gut, knocking him backward. He fell into the keyboards, almost toppling over, gasping for oxygen, and Seth grabbed at him, trying to steady him. His sudden concern only made things worse. A second surge slammed into Abaddon's senses. It was like wandering too far into the surf and getting smacked in the face with a wave. Abaddon reeled. He had to force himself to breathe and finally found his balance with one hand gripping the keyboard and the other arm tight around Seth's waist. His legs felt like rubber.

Other parts of him felt entirely too solid.

"Are you okay?"

Seth spoke into his ear, not wanting to disrupt the service, and Abaddon pulled away a bit, trying to put an inch of distance between them, trying to make his knees work. His hands shook. He forced himself to let go of Seth. He didn't have to force himself to smile though. He could still feel the jubilant energy their music had stirred between them.

"I'm fine."

"We make a great team! You almost kept up."

Abaddon laughed. "I think it's safe to say your soul still belongs to God." And as he said it, he felt the tiniest hint of relief.

And with that relief came a bit of shame.

He wanted Seth's soul. He hungered for the satisfaction that would come when he devoured it and delivered it through the abyss. But looking into Seth's smiling face, he felt the first hint of doubt. Abaddon had claimed a lot of souls over the years, most with a myriad of secret sins. Greed, jealousy, ambition. Those were the key to many a devil's success. Yet Seth had none of those things, and Abaddon knew the euphoric exhilaration he felt upon claiming Seth's soul would be matched only by the guilt he felt afterward.

Seth leaned toward him again. "I can't believe Zed let you get this close."

Abaddon laughed, trying to shake off his discomfort, and glanced over at the big, black foreman. He could have sworn he saw the rage of Heaven in the man's eyes. "I have no doubt he'd tear me limb from limb right now, if he could."

Seth smiled, the fingers of his left hand slipping easily into Abaddon's. The calluses on his fingertips from guitar and fiddle strings tickled across Abaddon's palm.

"Come on. We'll slip out the back way."

Abaddon's heart leapt. He swallowed, not sure he understood. "What?"

"My sense of direction gets all messed up in the tent, but I know it's there. Can you see it?"

"I know where it is." He'd watched Zed whisk Seth away through it the last few nights. He glanced toward Zed. He saw the man's understanding dawn, realizing Seth intended to escape his watch. "We better be quick," he said to Seth.

"I'm ready if you are."

Abaddon gripped Seth's hand tighter and led him off the stage, away from a fuming Zed, through the back door of the tent. They ran for the trees, both of them stifling their laughter like children as Abaddon led Seth through the shadows, away from the revival, deep into the heart of the woods.

Like all devils, he knew the path to temptation.

Once they were out of sight of the camp, they slowed to a walk. Abaddon still held Seth's hand. He loved the way it felt, that single point of contact where the warmth of Seth's soul could seep through his flesh, but now that they were away, he began to feel awkward about it. He let go, and immediately felt a sense of loss. He wasn't sure how much of the disappointment was his own and how much of it came from Seth.

"I'm glad you came on stage," Seth said, his voice hushed with shyness and uncertainty. "I thought you were there the last few nights, but Zed..." He laughed, shaking his head. "I'd ask him. He didn't want to tell me, but he wasn't willing to lie. So he'd say things like, 'Do not concern yourself with Abaddon's whereabouts, young Seth.'"

His mimicry of Zed's deep voice and stiff wording made Abaddon laugh. "He really does sound like Darth Vader, sometimes."

Seth's smile fell a bit. "I wouldn't know. I've never seen *Star Wars*. Or *Star Trek*. Whichever one that is."

"Not even before you went blind?"

Seth shook his head. "We don't see movies, or watch TV."

"Cell phones?"

"Definitely not. We barely even listen to the radio."

"Oh." Abaddon felt like an ass for inadvertently tainting Seth's bright mood. "Well, you aren't missing much. Just picture a big guy in a black cape flying around space in a giant basketball, killing his minions and occasionally blowing up planets."

"It sounds horrifying."

"It's possible I'm oversimplifying."

Seth stopped walking, turning to face Abaddon. He looked uncharacteristically somber, and Abaddon let his soul sense loose a bit, feeling for an explanation. Not too much. Not allowing himself to get a taste of that cotton-candy soul, because it would drive him mad. Just a quick flick of his senses like the tongue of a snake. The air around Seth was tainted with citrus, almost sour with loneliness and longing.

"Is something the matter?"

"We're leaving."

Abaddon blinked, surprised. "I thought you were staying through the end of the week, at least."

"I did too, but Brother Zed told me today we're hitting the road at dawn." He smiled, but it was the saddest smile Abaddon had ever seen. "We always seem to go just when I manage to make a friend. Sometimes I think he does it on purpose."

Abaddon took a step backwards, his thoughts a jumble. He'd come here for Seth's soul, but now, hearing Seth call him a friend, he felt another stab of doubt. "Do you know where you're going?"

"No. Zed won't tell me."

Abaddon frowned. *Sometimes I think he does it on purpose.* Abaddon didn't think Seth had been entirely serious, but he had to wonder if Seth had hit the nail right on the proverbial head. Zed clearly didn't trust Abaddon. Maybe they were moving just to escape him.

"It doesn't matter where you go. I'll find you. Zed can make you pack up and leave town, but there's no place on Earth he can hide you. Not from me."

Seth laughed. Even now, Abaddon could tell he didn't believe. He obviously thought Abaddon was making a joke. But then he sobered, his laughter giving way to a pained expression that almost looked like grief. "Is there a place we can sit down?"

The request surprised Abaddon. "Sure." He waved his fingers and produced a park bench out of the abyss. It'd disappear in a day or two, but it'd serve them just fine for now. "Here." He took Seth's arm and guided him to the bench, ready this time for the wave of power that washed over him.

Seth frowned as he sat, his hands tracing the wooden slats beneath him. "Was this already here? Out in the middle of nowhere?"

"No. I made it appear."

Seth chuckled again, shaking his head. "You're the strangest man I've ever met."

Abaddon was about to say, "I'm not a man," but Seth spoke again before he could.

"Can I tell you a secret?"

"Of course."

But now, having decided to tell Abaddon about whatever weighed on his conscience, Seth hesitated. It took him a minute to gather his thoughts and his courage. Abaddon sat next to him on the bench and waited until he finally began to speak.

"You asked me if my blindness was punishment. And I told you it wasn't, but…that might not have been the truth."

"Are you saying you lied?"

"No. It's just that when it comes to my blindness, sometimes I'm not sure what to believe."

"I don't understand."

"That's because I'm not explaining it well." He took a deep breath and changed course. "When I was eighteen, I decided to leave the revival."

"Oh? I was under the impression you loved it?"

Seth shrugged halfheartedly. "Most of the time, I do. I've had a good life here. I grew up in the revival. I was homeschooled by the Reverend's wife until she died, and then by the Reverend until he died. I've been surrounded by people who love me since the day I was found under that piano bench. I feel like I should be satisfied with what I've been given."

"But you aren't?"

Seth sighed, slumping a bit. "When I was eighteen, I realized..." He stopped again, biting his lip. Abaddon suspected Seth was fighting to keep from crying in front of him. "I'm alone here. I have friends, but I'm alone. And I'll always be alone because we don't stay anywhere long enough for that to change."

"But you have your brother. And that guy who plays the guitar. I see him talking to you all the time."

"Jeremy." Seth's voice was soft. "Yes, he's my friend. He has been since we were thirteen. But he has a wife. They all have wives and husbands. They care about me, but I'm not anybody's first priority. And sometimes, I think I'd really like to have somebody put me first."

"That's normal."

"Or maybe it's selfish."

Abaddon considered for a moment, wondering how this fit with Seth's initial confession of wanting to leave the revival. "You don't think you can find a wife amongst your Rainbowites?"

Seth shook his head. "I don't want a wife. And what I do want isn't the type of person who comes to bible-thumping revivals in Kentucky or Tennessee."

Abaddon hadn't expected that. "Are you telling me you're gay?"

Seth didn't reply, but the slow blush on his cheeks was answer enough.

"Are you worried it's a sin?"

Seth shook his head emphatically. "No. I know the conservatives think so, but that's not what I was taught. I was taught that love is never a sin, and that sex is only a sin if it's done outside the holy bonds of marriage."

"So you wanted to go find your soul mate?"

Seth slumped again. "You make it sound so stupid."

Abaddon frowned. That hadn't been his intent. "'Two are better than one. If two lie together, they keep warm, but how can one keep warm alone?'"

Seth laughed. "And suddenly you're the one quoting the bible?"

Abaddon found himself smiling at the absurdity of it. "I only meant that wanting an intimate partner in this life is natural."

Seth nodded, rubbing his palms on his jeans, seeming to gather courage from Abaddon's words. "We've never had TVs, or cell phones, or computers, but I've seen books and pictures. And when I was eighteen, I started making a list of places I wanted to go. I had a truck and my own trailer. I'd saved up a bit of money. I figured I didn't need much else. I was going to take my guitar and my violin, and just drive. Maybe go someplace where there were tourists, and play for pocket change. Just see what was out there, you know?"

Abaddon nodded, realizing too late that it did no good with Seth. "So what happened?"

"What happened was, I went blind. It was my nineteenth birthday, and when I woke up, I couldn't see. And later that day Zed joined our congregation, and he's been the one driving my truck ever since." Seth looked down again, gripping his hands in his lap. "All I wanted was to see a few things—the Grand Canyon. Maybe Zion National Park. I wanted to see the ocean." He wiped hurriedly at his eyes. "You asked what sin I'd committed to deserve being struck blind, and the thing is, there wasn't one. And yet I feel as if I've been punished all the same. But all I wanted was to see more of the world." He turned toward Abaddon, his face a mask of grief. "Is it wrong to want to witness the wonder of His creations with my own eyes?"

Abaddon almost wanted to cry for him. How could he tell Seth that despite his faith, God had probably had nothing whatsoever to do with him going blind? "There's nothing wrong with that at all. I think you were right the first time. This wasn't punishment. It was just really bad luck."

Seth wasn't bothering to hide his tears anymore. "So now I'm blind, and I'm stuck here, and I'll never see any of those things. I have to depend on others for everything. And I know I shouldn't feel sorry for myself, but sometimes…" He took a deep, shaking breath. When he spoke again, his voice was barely a whisper. "Sometimes I get so angry."

"That's a normal reaction."

"But a sinful one. And given the timing, I have to wonder. Maybe wanting to leave my brother is a sin. Maybe wanting to find somebody to share my life and my faith and my bed with is a sin too. Maybe—"

"No, Seth. None of those things are marks against you. I can see why your blindness might make you question what you've believed your whole life. I can see how you might start to read more into it than there really is. But believe me, they aren't related. There is no grand explanation. Sometimes the universe just doesn't play fair."

Seth sat there for a moment, staring blindly down at his lap, but Abaddon noticed that his eyes no longer brimmed with tears. "I can't decide if that makes me feel better or worse."

"Well, I was aiming for 'better', for what it's worth." Although he wondered at that. It wasn't in a devil's nature to be kind. "Look, I imagine going blind when you did probably felt like a kick in the balls. But it has nothing to do with you wanting to find the most simple, natural thing known to the human heart. I promise you that."

Seth sat a moment longer, pondering. Finally, he wiped his cheeks and gave Abaddon a weak smile. "Thank you."

"There's no need to thank me."

"There is, actually. Every other person I've tried to talk to about this has said the same stupid thing to me." His voice was uncharacteristically thick with disdain. "'God works in mysterious ways.'" He shook his head. "I know they mean well, but it doesn't help. But what you say makes me realize I'd rather believe in the unfairness of the universe than doubt the fairness of God."

Abaddon smiled. "And that's exactly why your soul is so damnably perfect."

They sat there for a minute longer. Seth's gratitude was like warm caramel on his wondrous soul, and Abaddon considered all the ways he might now try to bargain for it. Maybe offering Seth his sight again. Maybe offering to help him find a husband. Maybe simply taking him to the Grand Canyon to let him see its magnificence just once. It seemed so simple, and yet, he couldn't bring himself to do it. Seth had called him a friend, and Abaddon was reluctant to betray that simple trust.

In the end, he did nothing. And eventually, Seth sighed and stood. Abaddon followed suit.

"I should head back. Zed will be looking for me soon."

"I understand. Can you find the way back on your own?"

"Yes. I seem to have a knack for getting through the woods. It's the one consolation God has seen fit to grant me." He bit his lip, touching the scarf around his neck. "I'm not very good at saying goodbye."

"But this isn't goodbye. I meant it when I said I'd find you. Have faith in that, if nothing else. Besides, I still owe you ice cream."

"Yes, you do." Seth didn't believe him though. Abaddon felt no comfort coming off the boy. Only an echoing sense of loneliness and a touch of despair. Seth smiled, but his heart wasn't in it. He stepped forward, reaching for Abaddon, and for just a moment, Abaddon thought Seth was going to kiss him—not in a romantic way, but the simple Kiss of Peace his people used. Abaddon's heart swelled at the thought, but Seth stopped short. Instead, he touched Abaddon's forearm with the soft fingers of his right hand. One tiny touch, and yet it made Abaddon's vision blur and his heart pound.

"Peace and love to you, Brother Abaddon. You deserve it."

And now it was Abaddon's turn to feel like the universe had kicked him in the balls.

Chapter Five
Sympathy for the Devil

It took Abaddon three days lingering in the abyss with his senses prowling through the southeastern United States to find Seth and the Rainbow Revival again, but find them he did, tucked into a primitive campground near the Talladega National Forest in Alabama.

He drifted for a while in the darkness, keeping his eye on the campground. It was midmorning, and preparation for the revival was only beginning. Seth had yet to leave his trailer, and Abaddon waited in the abyss. He had less than a week left on his probation, but at least Zed would relax his guard now. After all, he'd put more than three hundred miles and the entire state of Tennessee between them and Kentucky. As far as he knew, he'd left Abaddon in Harlan County.

Finally, Seth emerged. He wore jeans and a T-shirt, but with one of his usual knit scarfs around his neck, and Abaddon reeled out his soul sense, letting it play over Seth's skin. Ah, the boy tasted as tempting as ever, even when tinged with a sense of loss, and Abaddon's fingertips tingled with excitement. He wanted to get closer. He wanted to feel that surge of electricity that came whenever they touched. He wanted to…

To…

Consume Seth's soul?

Yes.

And no.

He frowned, uncomfortable with his own indecisiveness.

Seth started across the campground toward the covered picnic pavilion where several of the group members were eating breakfast. He made it only a few steps though before he stopped in his tracks. He turned slowly to face the woods where Abaddon lurked.

Could Seth sense him?

Abaddon leapt from the abyss, materializing deep enough in the forest that he wouldn't be seen by Zed or the other revivalists. Seth's brow wrinkled, his eyes seemingly focused on some distant point near the treetops.

He took a cautious step in Abaddon's direction.

Yes. Perfect. Just keep walking.

A second step, then a third.

"Seth, where are you going?" Thaddeus called from the picnic pavilion.

Seth hesitated, and Abaddon felt his doubt. But he also felt a tiny spark of hope, deep in Seth's heart.

Trust yourself, he tried to say through whatever connection the two of them might share, desperate to somehow cast his lure through the many trees that stood between them and draw his prey closer.

"I'm just going for a walk. Don't worry."

Hidden in the trees, Abaddon smiled. He couldn't have planned it better if he'd tried. Seth strayed past the edge of the campground, stepping into the shade of the forest, and Abaddon's pulse beat a bit faster.

Yes, I'm here. Keep walking.

There was no way Seth should have heard him, and yet his steps became more confident, his uncanny ability to navigate blind in the woods working to his advantage. Five yards into the forest. Ten. Twenty-five, the ground now a thick layer of dried needles, the air pungent with the smell of pine. After forty yards, the campground was lost in the trees, and Seth came to a stop only three or four yards from Abaddon. Birds chirped. Leaves whispered in a faint breeze. Other than that, the forest was absolutely silent. Seth looked nervous. Even from where he stood, Abaddon could see that his hands shook as he rubbed his palms on his jeans.

Abaddon waited, uncharacteristically nervous as well, uncertain how to begin now that he'd succeeded in getting Seth alone.

Seth cleared his throat, then finally asked, in a croaking, uncertain voice, "Hello? Who's there?"

It was pretty much now or never.

"It's me."

Seth froze. His mouth opened and closed a couple of times before he managed, "Abaddon?"

"I thought you knew I was here. It was almost like you could see me."

"I— I don't know. I feel like I did, and yet..." He backed up a step, waves of fear wafting off of him for the first time. "I felt so stupid, because I thought I heard you, but..." He shook his head, taking another step backward. "This is all wrong. You shouldn't be here. You—"

"I told you I'd find you."

"Did you follow us?"

"Not exactly."

"Then how—"

"I don't travel the same way you do. Your soul—"

"Oh my gosh!"

"It's like a beacon to me, Seth. It's brighter than any lighthouse. It took me a couple of days to spot it, but once I did, I only had to follow its light here."

"Oh holy smoke!" Seth backed up again and ran into a tree, his strange not-quite sight in the woods failing him for the first time in Abaddon's presence. "Are you— Oh man, is this a joke, Abaddon? I want the truth now! Stop playing with me!"

"I told you the truth the first time I met you. I'm a devil."

"You can't be."

"But I am. Think about it. You knew I was here, didn't you? And how else could I have found you?"

"No." Seth shook his head again. Then, louder, "No! You're lying to me!"

"I'm not lying."

"But—"

"'And the Lord said unto Satan, Whence comest thou?'"

Seth took a deep breath, then another, finding strength in what he knew and understood. "'Then Satan answered the Lord, and said, From going to and fro in the Earth, and from walking up and down in it.'"

"Exactly."

"Oh, holy cow." Seth bent over, his hands on his knees, as if he might be sick. "I can't believe this is happening."

"I never lied to you about what I was."

"I figured it was a joke. Or maybe a metaphor. I don't know. Like you were warning me that you had unholy intentions."

Abaddon almost laughed. "'Unholy intentions'? What the hell does that mean?"

The tips of Seth's ears turned pink. "Nothing." He ran his fingers through his hair and stood straight. "What do you want from me? Are you here to kill me?"

"No. Nothing like that."

"Are you here to steal my soul?"

Abaddon hesitated, hating the twinge of guilt he felt. "Yes."

"I won't ever give it to you. Especially not now."

Abaddon feared that might be true. Part of him still hoped to change Seth's mind, but part of him rejoiced in the thought that Seth's soul might be out of reach. But how could he explain that to Seth when he barely understood it himself? "Maybe I just wanted to see you."

"But if you're a devil, you're probably lying to me. 'Ye are of your father the devil, and the lusts of your father ye will do.'"

Oh, how right he was. And yet how wrong, at the same time. "I was once a man like you, you know."

Seth's brow wrinkled in confusion. "You were?"

"I made a deal with the devil, just like you did the first time we met. The difference is, I lost."

"What did you bargain for? What did you want that was worth your soul?"

"I wish I knew." Abaddon tilted his head back, seeking the sky as if it could offer an explanation, but it was mostly lost in the dense trees. "I don't remember it. They take that all away when you cross over. But I know that's what happened."

"So you came for my soul originally, but you've decided now you don't want it?"

He sounded almost amused. Abaddon felt that twinge of guilt again, along with the weight of his unreached quota. How could he explain that he longed for Seth's soul the way a starving man craved food, and yet for the first time ever, he had the strength to deny his own need? "I don't want to hurt you."

One corner of Seth's mouth curved upward in a skeptical grin. "But you're a devil, right? I can't possibly trust you."

"You can." Abaddon felt the truth of the statement in some deep corner of his heart. "I couldn't say that about anybody else in the world, but I can't lie to you. You have some power over me I can't explain. You're brighter than the North Star, and the thought of extinguishing that…" He shook his head. "I want your soul, but I'm not sure I can do it. I'm not sure I could live with myself afterwards." And yet he'd have to, for all of eternity. There was no reprieve from Hell.

Seth considered that, his head cocked sideways. Abaddon waited, his heart in his throat. Finally, Seth said, "Huh."

After what had felt like a momentous admission, it was a surprisingly mundane response. "What does that mean?"

"I wish I could see you, so I could tell if you're laughing at me or not."

Power surged in Abaddon's heart, pulsing through his veins, down his limbs. His fingertips tingled with it. "I've laughed at you before when you threw bible verses at me," he confessed, his voice hoarse, "but not now. Not for this." He took one slow step toward Seth. Then another.

Seth must have heard him approach, because he backed up, holding up his hands as if to ward Abaddon off. "What are you doing?"

"I won't hurt you." He couldn't have, even if the rules allowed it. He was overwhelmed by the tenderness that filled him. There was something so wonderful about knowing that Seth knew him for what he really was, and yet seeing Seth still standing there, not asking for anything at all. Just waiting, as if having a little chat with a devil on a bright Sunday morning in the deep woods of Alabama was the most natural thing in the world.

Abaddon caught Seth's wrist to keep him still so he could move closer, reeling at the sensation that simple contact caused. Seth was trembling, and Abaddon stopped short, his fingertips an inch from Seth's cheek. "Are you ready?"

Seth's Adam's apple bobbed. When he spoke, his voice was tight. "For what?"

"You said you wished you could see me. Are you ready?"

"Wh-what?" Tears brimmed in Seth's eyes. "You can do that?"

But Abaddon didn't bother to answer. He couldn't. He couldn't think beyond the eagerness that filled him, being so near Seth and having a gift he could present, like some kind of offering. His throat was tight, and for a minute, he could only stare at Seth's trusting face. It was all he could do to keep from kissing him, pulling him close, sliding his hand inside Seth's shirt and feeling the soft skin of his lower back as they tasted each other.

But he resisted the urge.

He laid his palm against Seth's cheeks instead, the tips of his first two fingers on Seth's temple.

And he let the power flow.

It took only a second, and then Seth gasped. He didn't move his head—he held perfectly still—but his eyes moved rapidly, scanning back and forth, seeking a point of focus. "Ohh..." More tears pooled in his eyes, and finally, his gaze settled on Abaddon's face. "You weren't lying. I really can see."

It was hard to make his throat work. "Yes."

"Will it last?"

He could have done it in exchange for a soul, but as a favor? That simply wasn't allowed. He was already bending the rules. "No. I'm sorry. That's beyond my power."

"It's okay. This is enough. Just seeing the trees again is enough."

Seth looked around again, taking in the forest and the thin patch of sky and the sunlight dappling the ground before returning to Abaddon. Tears flowed freely down his cheeks, coming to rest on Abaddon's hand, where it cradled Seth's cheek. They felt like ice against his flesh, and yet he longed to feel more of them. He had a sudden and irrational urge to taste them. He moved his thumbs to wipe at them as best he could without breaking contact with Seth's temples.

"Oh, Abaddon," Seth said, his brow creasing with a frown. "Your eyes." He reached up with one hand and laid his fingers against Abaddon's cheek.

That tiny bit of contact made Abaddon's blood roar in his ears. He felt the full strength of Seth's soul in that touch. The purity of his heart. The undeniable weight of concern.

Concern for a devil.

Abaddon's mouth watered. The soul hunger stabbed all the way to his core. The urge to consume the boy whole, to drag him through the abyss and drink the sheer power that lingered in his heart was overwhelming, and Abaddon pulled away quickly, stumbling backward. He found himself bent over, hands on his knees, gasping for breath just as Seth had done earlier.

"What happened?" Seth asked.

Abaddon shook his head, then realized Seth was blind again. He couldn't see the gesture. "Nothing."

Seth took a cautious step toward him, his hand outstretched. Abaddon waited, practically holding his breath as Seth's fingers lit upon his shoulder. He felt the heat all the way through his shirt, the surge of temptation subsiding, but not fast enough.

"Will you come to the revival tonight?"

Abaddon laughed, the sound hoarse and grating in his throat. "Why?"

"'I have trusted in thy mercy; my heart shall rejoice in thy salvation.'"

The words burned. For the first time in his memory, Abaddon felt tears behind his eyes. "No. It's too late for me. You shouldn't even be talking to me. You should be running away from me as fast as you can."

"You said you wouldn't hurt me."

"I said I didn't want to hurt you. It's not the same thing."

Seth blinked, confused. "I don't understand."

"I know."

"You also said you wouldn't lie to me."

"And I won't."

"Then tell me what you mean."

Abaddon stood, stretching his back, pushing his hair roughly off his forehead. "If I were a man—a decent man—I'd leave you alone. But I'm not a man. I'm something much worse, and I'm required to hunt down certain things. And you…" He shook his head, wondering at the strength of his longing. "You're the epitome of those things. You have the purest soul I've ever encountered."

"That's something you can see?"

Abaddon nodded, even though the gesture was lost on Seth. "I can see it. I can smell it. I can even taste it, and goddamn it, Seth, it's the most tempting thing I've ever encountered. It's like I'm an addict, and you're the perfect fucking drug. I want both you and your soul." He took a step closer despite himself, his voice becoming thick and hoarse. "I hunger for you. In more ways than one."

A slow blush rose on Seth's cheeks. It only made him more tempting. "You can't take it without my permission though, right?"

The question surprised Abaddon. It felt like a sudden shift of direction. After giving voice to what he truly felt, confessing the strength and breadth of his desire, it was hard to back up and veer into a normal conversation as if nothing had happened. "Right. You'd have to agree."

"Do you intend to hurt somebody else? Somebody at the revival?"

"No. I told you the truth. I only wanted to see you. I just…" He shook his head, wishing he could explain it to himself so he'd know how to explain it to Seth. "You're amazing, in every way. I couldn't stay away."

Seth ducked his head, scuffing one toe in the dirt and leaves on the forest floor. "Will you come tonight? Please?"

"I can't be saved."

"That's not what I asked."

Abaddon sighed. He didn't want to give Seth false hope. On the other hand, the thought of sitting in the congregation and watching Seth play filled him with a lightness he hadn't felt in years. It also filled him with a pain he couldn't begin to define. "If it's what you want."

"It is."

"Until tonight then." Abaddon reached for Seth, but stopped short of allowing himself the contact. "Peace and love to you, brother." And for the first time ever, he meant it.

Chapter Six
Even Angels Dig the Doobies

If it hadn't been for the music, Abaddon might have grown tired of the revivals. They were all variations on the same speech. The same bible quotes used out of context. The same strange glances toward Seth as the collection plate filled. But listening to Seth play never got old. The band played the same songs from night to night, but they improvised a lot, jamming on the familiar riffs, allowing Seth and the choir room for ornamentation.

Abaddon found a seat on the right side of the tent, as he always did, about halfway between the stage and the entrance. He had a clear view of Seth at the keyboards for as long as the audience stayed sitting. His view was often blocked once people started standing, but that only impeded his eyes. Nothing could inhibit his soul sense, or the magic of Seth's music. And that night, he could have sworn Seth was playing just for him. The keyboard notes resonated against Abaddon's well of power. They crawled over him like a caress. They hinted at promises of things to come. It was the sweetest torture he'd ever endured, hungering for Seth's soul, even as he became more and more reluctant to claim it. Abaddon was both enraptured and impatient, loving the experience, yet counting the seconds until he might be able to steal a few moments alone with Seth, and so he didn't notice the commotion at first.

It started behind him, at the back of the crowd, just as the revival started to build toward the final act. It began with a low buzz of fear. Then, a woman screamed. For the first time ever, Seth's fingers missed a note, and Abaddon sat up, sensing Seth's sudden agitation, wondering what was wrong. The choir turned as one, not toward the disruption near the entrance of the tent, but toward Seth.

"Don't worry!" Thaddeus cried, stepping to the front of the stage and spreading his arms wide. "Let them pass! They won't hurt you!"

The murmurs from the crowd became more urgent, the hubbub moving like a wave up the rows. The Rainbow Revivalists moved quickly down the center aisle, standing on each side of it with their arms outstretched, holding the congregants back. People strained to see over them, to catch a glimpse of what all the fuss was about. Those close enough to see had wide eyes, their hands held to their lips.

"What is it?" people asked.

And then, Abaddon heard the word.

"Snakes!"

Snakes. The announcement rippled through the crowd, a breathless, enraptured whisper. *Bunches of them.*

"Let them pass!" Thaddeus called again. "They are sent by the Lord on this wondrous evening, so that we may witness the strength of my brother's devotion!"

Alarm flared in Abaddon's chest. He turned toward Seth. He'd stopped playing completely. He stood with his head bowed. He didn't look scared. He didn't look eager.

He looked resigned.

A choir member took his arm and guided him forward, to the front of the stage, and Abaddon caught the admiring glances the rest of the Rainbow Revivalists threw Seth's way.

This was what they'd been waiting for, watching Seth every night, hoping for this very thing. Abaddon stood on his chair, straining to see. What he saw made his heart burst into gear.

It was snakes, all right. Dozens of them. Easily as many as a hundred. Probably more. They slithered over each other in their eagerness, all of them moving with an inexplicable determination toward the front of the tent. There were rat snakes, Florida pine snakes, and corn snakes. Those were harmless enough, but mixed in among them, Abaddon spotted copperheads, cottonmouths, rattlers, and coral snakes, plus half a dozen other species that he couldn't identify on sight.

Seth descended the steps from the stage alone, undoing the top two buttons of his shirt as he did. He pulled the ever-present scarf from his neck and tucked it into his pocket, and the snakes surged forward.

Some of the congregants had followed Abaddon's example and climbed onto their chairs for a better view. Others pushed forward in their excitement. Seth sank to his knees, his arms stretching forward to the floor, as if to meet the wave of reptiles.

"Seth!" Abaddon yelled, but Seth couldn't hear him over the din of the crowd. A frantic glance around the tent at the other Rainbow Revival members alarmed him even more. None of them were moving to help. The choir was singing "I Stand Amazed". Thaddeus and Bob stood on the stage behind Seth, their eyes practically glowing with excitement. And Zed…

Zed stood to the side. He alone looked unhappy with the drama unfolding before them, but he didn't move to stop it.

The snakes went straight to Seth. They climbed his arms. They slithered into his lap. They writhed up his spine to wrap around his neck. The smaller ones circled around him, like a pack of wolves surrounding their prey.

"Seth!" Abaddon jumped off his seat, pushing the spectators out of his way. He shoved forward, determined to reach Seth before the snakes started biting, but the mortals were enraptured by the sight, frozen in their awe. He pushed harder, not caring if he knocked them over in his haste. He finally reached the aisle, but two of the Rainbow Revivalists blocked him, grabbing his arms to hold him back.

"Help him!" Abaddon screamed toward Zed.

Zed hung his head, looking almost ashamed.

"Goddamn it, let me go!"

But more of the Rainbow members had seen the struggle and moved forward to help subdue him. Seth was now lost beneath the snakes, only his hands and parts of his face visible. It was so unnatural, like something out of a bad horror movie, and Abaddon gritted his teeth. Power bubbled up from the well that resided where his soul used to be. It surged down his arms, tingled in his fingertips. He clenched his fists, debating the wisdom of using it against the mortals who held him.

"Brother Abaddon," Zed said, suddenly next to him. "I promise you, the boy will not be harmed."

"How can you say that? How can you just stand here and watch?"

"I appreciate your concern, but the phenomenon is almost over."

"The phenomenon?" Abaddon's anger flared again, this time directed at Zed, but when he looked toward Seth, he saw that Zed was right. As suddenly as they'd arrived, the snakes seemed to be losing interest in Seth. Those still on the ground headed for the door, as if they could read the glowing exit sign. The ones draped over Seth's body dipped toward the floor, abandoning their perch, fleeing for the Alabama woods.

The crazy thing was, of the Rainbow Revival members, only Seth and Zed looked relieved. The rest seemed strangely disappointed.

"What the hell?" Abaddon asked of nobody in particular. "What the fuck just happened?"

Thaddeus was already preaching again, shouting about how the righteous would be known by their ability to control serpents. Reverend Bob jangled his tambourine. The crowd raised their hands, crying out their praises. The collection plates appeared.

"It's over," Zed said quietly.

Seth pushed to his feet, pulling his scarf from his pocket. His friend Jeremy laid his guitar aside and came forward to take Seth's arm. He ducked his head close, conferring with Seth as the latter wrapped his scarf carefully around his neck. Then Jeremy took Seth's arm and began leading him toward the exit at the back of the tent.

Now that Abaddon had quit struggling and the "phenomenon" had ended, the revivalists released him. Zed caught the direction of Abaddon's gaze and sighed.

"I'll give you a minute with him, but you are not to enter his living space, Brother Abaddon. I still do not trust you, and I urge you not to overstay your welcome."

Abaddon was almost as stunned by Zed's sudden acquiescence as he had been by the snakes. "I won't. Thank you."

Abaddon ducked through the crowd and hurried for the exit. Seth and Jeremy were halfway across the clearing to Seth's trailer when Abaddon caught up with them. Seth was paler than usual, his eyes drawn and tired. After what he'd seen, it was all Abaddon could do to not grab him and pull him into his arms, but with Jeremy there, it seemed like a bad idea. He settled for taking Seth's hand, feeling that surge of power that always came with skin-to-skin contact. "Are you all right?"

Seth only smiled, although it never reached his eyes. It was Jeremy who spoke.

"Peace and love to you, brother. You must be Abaddon. We haven't actually met, but I've been hearing a lot about you."

Abaddon had to let go of Seth to shake Jeremy's hand. His was another bright, pure soul—one that might have tempted Abaddon greatly not so very long ago—but he paled next Seth.

Every star in the universe paled next to Seth.

"Can I talk to you for a minute?"

Seth's soft smile seemed a little more genuine this time. "Of course."

But Jeremy shook his head. "It'd be better to let him rest. The snakes always tire him—"

"I'll be fine, Jeremy. Abaddon will see me the rest of the way home."

Abaddon had to wonder what Zed had told Jeremy, because the boy seemed reluctant to leave them alone, but he grudgingly deferred to Seth's wishes, and Abaddon finally had Seth to himself.

"They all treat me like a recalcitrant child. As if my blindness is somehow my way of rebelling against them."

"I think they're only concerned for your welfare."

Seth laughed. "Funny how you're the one who gives them the benefit of the doubt." He gestured behind him, toward his trailer. "Do you want to come in, or—"

"No. I promised Zed I wouldn't." He might have thumbed his nose at Zed's rules in the past, but he felt compelled to follow them now. "Can we just walk?"

"Certainly."

Abaddon led him past the trailers, into the trees, into the deep darkness of the trees. There was no moon. Very little light reached them, but between Seth's blindness and Abaddon's unnatural vision, neither of them needed it, and it would help hide them from the eyes of curious revivalists. Seth followed easily, whether based on the sound of Abaddon's steps or something else entirely, Abaddon didn't know.

Abaddon clenched and unclenched his fists. His shoulders were so tight his head was beginning to ache. He wasn't sure what he felt—anger, or grief, or just confusion. The urge to take Seth and run as far away as possible was almost tangible. The revival no longer felt safe.

"You're troubled," Seth said at last.

Troubled. It seemed like such a tiny, silly word compared to the chaos he'd felt as he'd watched the serpents climb up Seth's pale, slender arms.

"What were you thinking?" Abaddon asked, turning to face him. "You could have been bitten."

Seth shrugged, as if it were inconsequential. "I could have, yes. But I wasn't."

"You could have died!"

A darkness passed over Seth's face. He touched the scarf around his neck. "Probably not."

Suspicion bloomed in Abaddon's heart. He'd never once seen Seth without something wrapped around his neck. Years earlier, he'd met a man with a similar tendency, but that man had made a hobby of hanging himself from the towel bar in his bathroom while he masturbated. He wore turtlenecks and scarves to hide the rope burn.

Abaddon couldn't picture Seth asphyxiating himself, but he was suddenly sure that scarf was hiding something.

He moved closer, dread pooling in his gut. Seth jumped when Abaddon's fingers touched his neck. But then Seth closed his eyes and held very, very still as Abaddon unwrapped the length of twisted silk. What he saw made his heart clench. Tiny, round scars, all in sets of two. There were a few in front, and Abaddon was sure if he looked, he'd find more in the back, but they were thickest on the sides, the glistening scar tissue trailing from just above Seth's collarbone to just beneath his ears.

"Holy hell, Seth. How many times have you been bitten?"

Seth shrugged again, taking the scarf from Abaddon's hand. "I don't know. A lot."

Abaddon touched one of the scars, electricity and power tingling through his fingers. For the first time, Seth seemed to feel it too. His breath hissed through his teeth and he jerked his head away.

"Always on your neck?"

A slow blush began to creep up Seth's cheeks. "No. All over. My neck and my chest and my stomach and...my thighs." His cheeks were now bright red, his words barely a whisper. "All over my thighs, but especially, you know. Up high."

"It doesn't hurt?"

Seth kept his eyes averted but didn't answer.

"Why aren't you dead?"

Seth shook his head. Abaddon waited, and eventually, Seth cleared his throat and spoke. "'And when Paul had gathered a bundle of sticks, and laid them on the fire, there came a viper out of the heat, and fastened on his hand. And the barbarians said among themselves, no doubt this man is a murderer who vengeance suffereth not to live. But Paul shook off the beast into the fire, and felt no harm. And they looked when he should have swollen, or fallen down dead suddenly: but after they had looked a great while, and saw no harm come to him, they changed their minds.'"

He hadn't finished the verse though, so Abaddon finished it for him. "'And they said that he was a god.'"

Seth didn't reply.

"Are you telling me you're a god?"

Seth jumped as if he'd been slapped. "No! No, that's not it at all. I just know that sometimes they come. And sometimes they bite me. And when they do, I can—" He stopped short.

"You can what?"

Seth took a deep breath, squaring his shoulders. "I can heal people."

"What?" He'd thought Seth's sect was different from the bible-thumping, faith-healing groups, but now... "Are you shitting me?"

"I know it sounds crazy, but the snakes—"

"They could kill you!"

"No! In Mark it says—"

"I know what it says in Mark, and in Luke." They were the verses Thaddeus had quoted after the "phenomenon", the same verses the serpent-handlers always pointed to, justifying their belief that handling venomous snakes proved their righteousness. They were utter bullshit as far as Abaddon was concerned.

"Seth..."

But he had no idea what to say. He couldn't describe what he felt as he imagined those fangs sinking into Seth's flesh. He touched the scars again, and this time, Seth didn't pull away. He closed his eyes and stood, unmoving, as Abaddon's fingers traced the marks. He wanted to touch each one. To heal them, even though it was against the rules. Seth's pulse pounded beneath his fingers. His breathing became shallow, and Abaddon's supernatural senses detected the sudden longing that blossomed in Seth's heart. The twinge of arousal in his loins. The undeniable joy at being as close as they were. The knowledge made Abaddon ache in the most wonderful, horrible way, and he pulled away, taking a step backward before he did something foolish.

"You're Abaddon," Seth said, his voice a shaky whisper. "But are you *the* Abaddon? The Destroyer?"

Abaddon was glad to have something to take his mind off his desire, and off the fact that Seth apparently felt the same way. "Angel of the Abyss, you mean? King of the Army of Locusts?"

Seth finally turned his blind eyes toward Abandon's face. "Are you?"

"No. I'm not him. When we cross over, they make us choose a name, but there aren't that many to choose from. Mammon, Azazal, Beelzebub, Mestama. Maybe a dozen more. They added Damien in the seventies, thanks to Hollywood." He laughed, although it came out wrong. "We have it better than the women though. They only have three: Lilith, Lamashtu, and Lamia. They petition to add Delilah every few decades, but it never passes."

"But does the real Abaddon exist?"

Abaddon blinked, surprised by the question. "I don't know. Probably, I guess."

"And Satan? Have you met him? Or God?"

"I've never seen either one of them in person."

"But you know they're real?"

Abaddon wasn't sure he liked where this was going. "I guess."

"And if devils are real, then angels must be too, right?"

"Oh, sure." He was glad they'd moved away from God. "Angels are real."

"Have you seen them?"

"Well, devils only see angels if the angel wants to be seen. They can hide from us, although we can't hide from them. They always know us on sight, although I'm not sure how. But I've met a couple over the years. I ran into Hadraniel at Sturgis once, and I sat next to Ambriel at a Doobie Brothers concert."

"Who are the Doobie Brothers, and what's a sturgis?"

Abaddon laughed. "Never mind. It doesn't matter."

Seth nodded, but Abaddon could tell his thoughts were elsewhere. "I think it must be your eyes that give you away."

"What do you mean?"

"Earlier, when you let me see you…"

"Yes?"

"Your eyes were wrong. They were…empty. And I don't mean that in some poetic way. I mean, they were utterly black. I could see the abyss in them."

"Oh." Abaddon touched each eyelid with a fingertip. They felt normal enough to him. Then again, he didn't really remember what they'd felt like before he'd crossed over. "I didn't know."

"That must not be how the others see you though. The girls keep teasing me, telling me how it's unfair to waste somebody as good-looking as you on a man who can't even see him. But they never mention your eyes being wrong."

There were too many pieces of that confession that intrigued Abaddon. His fathomless eyes, and Seth being teased as if they were a couple, and…

"What exactly do you tell them about me? How did you explain me finding you all the way in Alabama?"

"I told them the truth, but I let them think it's a joke. They all guess, and when they come up with something that sounds reasonable, I give a vague answer, like, 'Yeah, that's about right.'"

Abaddon found himself smiling. "So you don't have to lie?"

"Not outright, at any rate. The general consensus is that you lost your job and your house and maybe your wife, and now you're living out of your car. They all think you're following me around because you've fallen in love with me. It's easier to let them believe that than to tell them you just like the flavor of my soul."

There was a question buried in the statement—one that made Abaddon squirm a bit, his insides feeling somehow too light for his body. "I wonder why you could see me the way they can't."

Seth frowned. "Probably because it was you who gave me my sight. Like I was seeing you through your eyes."

Now it was Abaddon's turn to frown. That didn't make sense to him, but Seth spoke again before he could think on it further.

"You told me that you were once a man."

Abaddon's heart clenched. He didn't want to talk about this either. "Yes."

"When?"

Abaddon rubbed his hand over his forehead. Overhead, the stars blazed, but here, they were lost in the shadow of the trees. Abaddon suddenly longed for wide-open spaces and brilliant skies as far as the eye could see. He halfway debated whisking Seth off to the Grand Canyon, simply because he could.

"I don't know. I might have died in World War I." He based his guesses on his oldest memories as a devil, but they were vague and surreal. The only solid thing that ever came to him was the horrifying feeling of icy cold water filling his throat and lungs. "I think maybe I drowned."

"I bet you were a good man."

Abaddon closed his eyes, burying his face in his hands. "Seth—"

"There was a boy once." Seth still held his scarf, and he twisted it nervously between his hands. "We were in Alabama, near Mobile. He came to every revival, and every time he'd stay after and talk to me."

He kept his head lowered as he spoke, and Abaddon waited for him to go on.

"I was eighteen. I could still see, back then. And I'd stand in the greeting line at the beginning of the revival. I'd count where he was in line, and I'd make sure I was the one to greet him."

"The Kiss of Peace? Is that the greeting you're talking about?"

Seth raised his head at last, and in that dim place among the trees, Abaddon could have sworn Seth could see him.

"Whenever he kissed me, I was filled with the most glorious light. It was like nothing I'd ever felt, like I could sprout wings and fly. And one night, I dreamed that I lay beneath him. I dreamed of his lips and of his touch, and when I woke, the snakes had come. My bed was full of them. They were wrapped around me, around my arms and my legs and around..." Abaddon waited, practically holding his breath. "Around all of me. It was as if time had slowed, and their bites were caresses. I could feel their fangs sinking into my flesh, into my neck and the insides of my thighs, and I could feel their venom pumping into my veins. And holy cow, Abaddon, it was the most exquisite thing I've ever felt."

Abaddon had a hard time making his voice work. "Why are you telling me this?"

"Because that's how I feel when I'm with you."

It was as if Seth had cast his line into the water, and now reeled it in. Abaddon hadn't felt the hook tear into his flesh, but he didn't mind being caught. He felt the same wondrous exhilaration Seth was describing, and hearing Seth put it into words was more than he could stand. Abaddon pulled him close, one arm around his waist, one hand on his slender neck.

Seth's breath caught in his throat. He clutched the front of Abaddon's shirt. "Are you going to kiss me?"

"You're damned right, I am."

The first touch of his lips against Seth's nearly blinded him. The power of Seth's soul washed over him, sinking through his flesh, drowning his senses, and for the first time, Abaddon didn't pull away from that power. He sank deeper into it, holding Seth tighter, running his tongue gently over Seth's lips until the boy parted them and let him inside. Their tongues met, just barely. A soft moan rose from Seth's throat, a quiet, breathless sound of wonder that went straight to Abaddon's groin, and then Seth wrapped his arms round Abaddon's neck and gave himself up entirely to Abaddon's kiss.

He tasted exactly as Abaddon had known he would— like cotton candy and warm honey—and Abaddon savored that sweetness, sinking deeper into this new blissful torture he'd found. The earth might shatter. The sky might rip in two. Demons could pour forth from the earth and fire rain down from the heavens, and Abaddon wouldn't have seen it. He was lost in Seth's brilliance, high on his purity, enraptured by his taste. He hadn't felt anything like it in all the years since passing over, and if he'd felt it before losing his soul, he didn't remember and didn't care. He felt sure that anything from his past must pale next to this.

Satan may own his soul, but the rest of him was putty in Seth's sweet, devout hands.

But Abbadon was still a devil. Maybe the hunger to consume Seth's soul had abated, but only because it had been replaced by desires that were far more base and equally unholy. Another minute of this bliss and he'd start tearing off Seth's clothes, so he broke their kiss, but not their embrace, breathing hard. Seth's lips were damp, parted in eagerness, and Abaddon moaned at the sight.

"Oh, Abaddon," Seth breathed. "Is this what sin feels like? Because up until now, I never understood why it was so hard to resist."

"This is only the beginning. The things I could teach you about sin…" And he wanted to. Man, did he want to. But it would be the most horrific thing he'd ever done. "I shouldn't be doing this. You're the most innocent person I've ever met—"

"I don't care about 'innocent'. I wanted you to kiss me. I still want you to kiss me."

"Seth." He spoke clearly, emphasizing each word, hoping to drive his point home. "I am the devil."

"You're a devil, not *the* devil, right? That's what you told me."

"But I am temptation. Don't you see? I am the serpent in your garden, made flesh."

"I don't care."

"You should care. You should be running from me as fast as you can. You should be terrified."

"'There is no fear in love—'"

"No, don't start with the bible quotes!"

"'—but perfect love casteth out fear: because fear hath torment. He that feareth not is made perfect in love.' Don't you see? It applies to us both."

"No, Seth, it doesn't. I wish it did but—"

Seth kissed him again. There was no hesitancy at all. No fear or uncertainty, despite his inexperience. There was only joy at finally being given the thing he wanted most, and the natural urge to do more. To touch more. To share more. The flavor of his soul fluxed and changed, his arousal adding a hint of cinnamon and smoke to his cotton-candy and honey sweetness, and it was still so fucking perfect and deliciously tempting that Abaddon whimpered, wavering, torn between doing what was right and doing what they both wanted. He couldn't say yes, but he sure as hell couldn't say no. Not when he could feel Seth's hands in his hair. Not when he could taste the urgency that pounded in Seth's heart and burned in his groin.

They'd both be lost forever if they went down this path.

"Seth? Where are you?"

It was Zed's voice, ripping through the trees, tearing Seth from his arms, leaving Abaddon off-balance and weak-kneed. Seth was bent over, his hands on his thighs, the red scarf like a flag, trailing from the fingers of his left hand. He took a couple of ragged, gasping breaths. He stood and stuffed the scarf into his jeans pocket, his hands shaking. When he spoke, his voice was hoarse and thick with the same arousal that thrummed through Abaddon's veins. "I have to go."

"I know."

"Tell me you'll come back tomorrow."

"There's nothing in Hell or on Earth that could keep me away."

He just had to hope Heaven stayed out of the equation.

Chapter Seven
On the ~~Highway~~ Subway to Hell

Abaddon returned to Hell that night. He could have lingered near the revival, drifting in the abyss, out of sight of human eyes but near enough to keep an eye on Seth, but eventually, even devils needed rest.

And he needed time to think.

His apartment felt smaller than ever. Tenements in Hell had one window, all with a spectacular view of a brick wall six inches away. Sounds echoed through the hallways at all hours of the night—screaming, pounding, radios turned up too loud. Sometimes the sounds of babies crying, even though no infants resided in Hell. Sometimes dogs barked or roosters crowed, even though no Earthly animals resided in Hell either. Sometimes the Hounds of Hell brayed all night, chasing some doomed prey. The clamor changed every other week or so, in an effort to keep the locals from growing complacent. Still, after a few decades, there wasn't much that could surprise Abaddon.

He couldn't blame his lack of sleep on Hell.

He turned the revival and the snakes over and over in his mind, picturing the scars on Seth's neck. He considered the unnatural brightness of Seth's soul, and his claim of being able to heal people.

There was something going on here. Something Abaddon hadn't quite recognized until now. He needed to talk to Baphomet, and the only way to do that was to go back to work.

Traveling on the mortal plane was easy, but by design, traveling in Hell was…well, it was hell. The subway stunk, as usual. The exact odor varied from day to day, but it was never pleasant. Today's aroma seemed to be a blend of vomit and rotting fish. Also as usual, there were no seats available. They were all taken by mimes, surly teenagers, or large purses that bit your hand if you tried to move them. The one unoccupied seat contained a noxious puddle that was undoubtedly the source of the stink du jour.

Abaddon hung onto the overhead loop and wished for a cup of coffee.

When he finally reached his office, he took the stairs to the hundred and thirty-second floor (the elevator was always broken). He had to stop to catch his breath midway up, even after all these years. His luck was with him, though. He found Baphomet almost immediately. He was at his desk with a three-foot-high stack of "You're pre-approved!" announcements, ready to be folded and stuffed into envelopes. And when it came to sealing envelopes in Hell, there were no shortcuts. Each envelope flap had to be licked by some poor devil.

Baphomet put the most recent envelope aside and looked up with a smile. "Abaddon! Where have you been?"

"Topside." Abaddon scrubbed his fingers through his hair as he glanced around, making sure no managers were nearby. Most of the cubicles around them were empty, so he grabbed a chair and pulled it up next to Baphomet's desk.

"What in the world are you doing?" Baphomet asked, his voice an urgent whisper as he leaned toward Abaddon. "You're already on probation. If they catch you—"

"Yeah, yeah." Abaddon patted the air, trying to quiet his friend, even though they were already speaking in hushed tones. "Listen, I need to talk to you."

"Is this about that perfect soul you're trying to bag?"

Abaddon winced, hating the way it sounded. "It's about Seth, yes."

Baphomet lowered the envelope he'd been about to lick. "Oh no."

"What?"

"The way you said his name just now." He shook his head. "Abaddon, you need to stop seeing him. Nothing good can come of this."

"Will you shut up and listen to me?" At least that question didn't have to be whispered. It was okay to sound angry. He grabbed the top two inches of papers off the top of Baphomet's pile and began folding them, happy to have something to concentrate on while he talked. "Last night, I watched a goddamn river of snakes slither up the center aisle of a revival, like the motherfucking Pied Piper was leading them."

"The motherfucking Pied Piper led rats, not snakes."

"Whatever. They went straight up the aisle and straight to…" He had to take a deep breath and focused on the paper in his hands. Fold the top third down. The bottom third up. Add it to the stack waiting to be stuffed into envelopes and move on to the next form. "Straight to Seth. They swarmed all over him, like bees on honey."

"I'm not sure bees actually—"

"Listen to me! They crawled up his arms and into his lap and around his neck. He was covered. It was like nothing I've ever seen."

"Did they bite him?"

"No, but apparently they have before. I saw the scars. He's probably been bitten nearly a hundred times over the years."

Baphomet sat still, a folded form in one hand and an empty envelope in the other. "Was he controlling them?"

"I don't think so, no. But he says they come sometimes. He'll wake up with them in his bed."

Baphomet paled. "Abaddon, that's not human."

"There's more." He glanced around again, making sure nobody was nearby. "When I asked him which instruments he could play, he said, 'All of them.' And I think he meant it, although he's better at some than others. And I have this feeling he can see me. He's blind, but I swear, he senses me. He can follow me through the woods. His eyes always find me in the crowd. And when I granted him sight—"

"You gave him sight without trading for his soul? You know that's against the rules!"

"It was only for a second. My point is, he said my eyes were wrong. He said he could see the abyss in them. And he says…. Well, he says he can heal people."

Baphomet hadn't moved. "Is that all?"

"No." He was hesitant to say the last bit, but it seemed important. "He says when the snakes bite him, it's…"

"Arousing?"

Abaddon jerked his head in a nod.

"Hell's bells."

"What does it mean?"

Baphomet swallowed, his eyes wide. He set his forms aside and steepled his fingers, thinking. "The music doesn't tell us much. The ability to play any instrument with adequate skill could come from either an angel or a devil."

"And the ability to play some of them exceptionally well?"

Baphomet waved his hand dismissively. "Pure human tenacity and a lot of practice."

"What about the rest?"

"Well, angels can heal. You know that. Devils can too, but only in exchange for a soul. And being able to see you as you really are? That's definitely an angelic trait."

Abaddon heard the "but" coming. He waited for Baphomet to go on.

"On the other hand, snakes have been connected to Satan since the Garden of Eden. Angels may be immune to their venom, but they don't enjoy it."

"But he has a soul." Not just any soul, either. A soul that burned hot as the sun against Abaddon's devilish senses. "That means he can't be an angel, or a devil."

"Angels don't have souls, but you know as well as I do that devils can't ever detect that lack of soul. It's part of how they stay hidden from us."

"Yes, but I've met angels. They may throw up some kind of blinder—"

"It's more like a decoy."

"Fine. A decoy then. But it's never strong. It always feels common. Pedestrian. It's designed not to attract attention. But Seth's soul…" He shook his head. "Believe me, it's extraordinary."

Baphomet nodded, scratching his chin. "So how can this boy have a soul, yet display traits of both angels and devils? That's the question."

Abaddon's head jerked up. Their eyes met, both of them reaching the same conclusion at the same time.

"No," Abaddon said, shaking his head. "How could an angel and a devil reproduce together?"

Baphomet looked amused. "In the usual way, I suppose. If they were in human form, there's no reason they couldn't do a little horizontal tango."

"Could it have been rape?"

Baphomet frowned. "I don't see how. No devil could rape an angel. They're stronger than us. And no angel would rape a devil, because angels just don't do that kind of thing. Rape is, you know, pretty un-angelic, any way you look at it."

"And regardless of which one was the victim, they could always just give up their human form and return to Heaven."

"Or to Hell."

"Right."

"And one more thing you're forgetting." Baphomet put his elbows on the desk and leaned closer. "Both of them had to be in human form when the baby was conceived, but a human pregnancy is forty weeks long. Whichever one of them was the mother, she chose to remain on the mortal plane that entire time. She could have returned to the abyss, or to Heaven, and that would have been the end of it. But she chose to have that baby." He leaned back, picking up another of Abaddon's folded papers and stuffing it into an envelope. "Sounds like love to me."

Could it be true? And if so, what did it mean?

Maybe nothing.

Maybe everything.

"One thing's for certain," Baphomet said, interrupting his thoughts. "If he has a soul, you're right. It's probably worth a promotion, at the very least."

Abaddon's heart sank. "Yeah. Great."

"So get back up topside and claim it already."

The trip to Hell took far longer than he intended. The revival had already started by the time he returned to the mortal plane. Even with the band playing and Thaddeus preaching, Seth looked up when Abaddon walked in, his blind eyes seeming to find him as he claimed an empty seat near the back. It seemed Abaddon's presence tickled Seth's angelic senses, the same way Seth's mortal soul teased his. Abaddon felt the way Seth's heart skipped into a quicker tempo. He tasted the warmth that spread through the boy's chest. He closed his eyes and savored the undercurrent of longing that flowed over him. Seth's quiet joy at Abaddon's presence seemed to caress him, whispering of trust and devotion, the tang of his soul made sweet and syrupy by the sheer innocence of Seth's heart.

How could Abaddon betray that?

Was it possible those currents flowed both ways? Maybe Seth detected Abaddon's turmoil. Maybe he knew how much Abaddon struggled, torn between his ridiculous feelings for Seth and the knowledge that his probation was almost up. He had only a few days left. If he didn't meet his quota, he'd be stuck in Hell forever, far enough away that even Seth's light wouldn't reach him.

He had to act now, but the thought of trying to bargain for Seth's soul again almost made him sick to his stomach. Seth deserved better than that. But if he was too sentimental to do what needed to be done, what in the world was he doing here at all? He needed to be someplace else, looking for victims. He was being reckless and stupid staying here, gambling on the Holy Grail of souls when he could have been bagging half a dozen actors or athletes, but he couldn't help himself. Nobody excited him the way Seth did. No regular mortal soul would be enough to satisfy his hunger. And so even though it was foolish, Abaddon didn't leave. He stayed rooted to his chair, watching Seth.

Thinking.

He was so lost in his thoughts he didn't hear the commotion begin near the door of the tent. He became aware of the snakes not because of the tumult from the crowd, but because the flavor of Seth's soul suddenly shifted, becoming both smokey and bitter as excitement warred with a surprising abundance of fear and anxiety.

Why was he afraid?

Seth left the keyboard, pulling his scarf from his neck and tossing it aside as he descended the steps. The snakes surged toward him. Abaddon rose to his feet, trying not to be alarmed.

The congregants were all moving toward the center aisle, some of them standing on their chairs, anxious for a view. Zed stood in his usual place at the foot of the stage, on the right-hand side, ready to head Abaddon off if he tried to reach Seth. But now, with Seth in the center aisle, he was closer than ever.

Abaddon went the other way. He jumped over the river of snakes and crossed all the way to the far side of the tent, working his way slowly up the left-hand aisle to the front of the tent. Zed watched him, his eyes hard and angry. Abaddon held up both hands, doing his best to look innocent.

It wasn't something devils excelled at.

He didn't approach Seth though. He found a place where he had a clear view, but stayed back and watched.

The snakes swarmed up Seth's arms and legs, just as they'd done the night before. They moved slowly over Seth's flesh, sliding seductively under his shirt, their tongues tickling his soft skin, caressing him, whispering songs of seduction into his ear. Abaddon felt Seth's fear begin to drain away, fading beneath the surge of desire that filled him. It poured off him so strong Abaddon wondered that no other devils or angels poked their heads into the tent to investigate. It was a delicious tang of arousal and longing mixed with the bitter acceptance of shame and surrender. It was a taste devils knew well. It was the seductive blend of men unbuttoning their jeans and sliding their hands inside, torn between arousal and embarrassment at their baseness. It was the secret thrill some women felt as they wedged a pillow between their legs and began to move, hoping the kids didn't hear. It was pure sexual energy, but with a tantalizing hint of guilt.

The first bite came slowly. Not a fast, lunging strike, but an exquisite nudge, fangs easing into the flesh at the base of Seth's neck like a groom between his bride's virgin thighs, pushing deeper, strength and tenderness driving for some wondrously sensitive spot. Then another snake, on the opposite side. A third, nearer his ear, pumping venom sinfully into Seth's veins. Then more of them, the strikes coming faster, rattlers with tails thrashing, the hissing of the multitude becoming a moan, all of them writhing in their excitement, biting over and over, driving toward some unknown release.

Seth cried out, his arms flung wide. Abaddon wondered if he and Seth were the only men in the room whose cocks were hard and erect. He wondered if any of the women in the tent were hot and wet between their legs.

The snakes began to leave, slow and listless now, as if they'd been sated too. Seth rose slowly to his feet, blood running in narrow streams down his pale neck, blossoming in patches on his white shirt from the bites on his stomach and back. Pricks of red lined the inside of his pant legs. He turned slowly to his left. His eyes never gained focus. They stared into some unknown place, but he held out a hand and moved forward, his steps slow and sure.

"Let him pass!" Thaddeus cried into the sudden silence. Even the band and the choir had stopped. Everybody watched Seth with the same bated breath. "My brother is searching for somebody special now. Let him by. Make room for him."

He needn't have bothered telling them. The congregants shrank from Seth as he neared, backing up hurriedly as if he might bite like one of his snakes. He moved down the third row of chairs, finally stopping in front of a middle-aged woman. He held out a hand to her.

"I can heal you."

Fingers flew to shocked lips. The woman's eyes went wide and she sank into a chair. "What? B-but I'm not sick."

She was though. Abaddon let his senses crawl over her, and knew immediately what Seth had obviously sensed as well. Cancer lurked in her breasts and ovaries. It crawled toward her uterus. It reached slender, treacherous fingers toward her heart and lungs. It was like bitter dark chocolate on Abaddon's tongue, thick and heavy. He might have pegged her as a prime target, if he hadn't been too focused on Seth to notice the souls of mere mortals.

"You are," Seth said, his voice gentle. "You've suspected for a while, but you've been too afraid to make an appointment." He moved closer, his fingers brushing her hair away from her temple, soothing her like a mother would a child. "It's okay, though. I can make you better."

The woman closed her eyes. The crowd around them took a tiny step forward. Seth placed both hands on her head.

There wasn't much to see. There was no chanting. No praying. None of the theatrics Abaddon had come to associate with faith healers. Seth simply stood there, stock-still, his head bowed.

But Abaddon didn't have to rely on his eyes.

Seth was no charlatan. He really could heal. Abaddon felt the slender tendrils of sickness in the woman's body begin to wither. He stood amazed as unhealthy cells died and were reborn healthy. The chocolate tang of her soul receded, becoming bland and dull as iceberg lettuce. Death was receding. Fear was dying.

But that wasn't all.

Seth's soul was changing as well. The brilliance that had nearly blinded Abaddon from the beginning flared and raged. It burned inside Seth's slender chest, so bright and horrifying that Abaddon closed his eyes, hoping it would help.

It didn't.

Seth let the woman go and moved quickly past her, pushing through the crowd, back to the center aisle. He made his way down it, stumbling as if he was drunk. He found a man, his lungs black and riddled with disease. Beads of sweat bloomed on Seth's forehead, dripping past his temples to mix with blood and venom on his neck. Seth laid his hands on the man's shoulders and stood there, not moving, forcing the man's lungs to turn pink until they filled with oxygen in a way they hadn't done in forty years.

Seth stumbled on again, his face a sickly shade of gray, his soul blazing so hot Abaddon wondered that the tent didn't ignite. Abaddon pushed through the crowd, needing to be closer. Zed did as well.

Nobody else moved.

Seth fell to his knees at the feet of an old woman, stooped with arthritis and pain.

"I can help."

It was barely a whisper, but it carried through the silent tent. Seth took her gnarled hands in his. He lowered his head, laying his forehead on them. His bony shoulders shook. Even on his knees, it seemed it was all he could do to stay upright. But the woman's pain receded. Her shoulders rose. Her back straightened. When Seth released her hands, her fingers were perfect, her knuckles shrunk to regular size.

The people close enough to see gasped. This was the first healing they could see with their mortal eyes.

Seth rose shakily, his face almost skeletal, his pallor edging toward green. His soul glowed. It pulsed. It seemed to scorch Abaddon's flesh like a bonfire. The overwhelming sweetness was almost sickening, even to him.

All that disease. All that pain. None of it was gone. Seth had absorbed it all, soaking it into his supernatural cells.

Seth turned, stumbling up the aisle. The crowd parted to let him pass. He staggered straight to Abaddon and collapsed. Abaddon caught him, for all the good it did. The strength of Seth's soul was like a fist into his solar plexus and he fell to his knees, gasping, Seth's limp body in his arms.

"You're dying." The realization made him reel. It filled him with a helplessness he'd never known. "Goddamn it, why didn't you tell me you were dying?" He held Seth tight, letting his senses dig deeper and deeper into Seth's body, following the path of his cells, finally seeing what he'd been too blind to see before. "That's why you burn so bright. That's what makes you so perfect. Goddamn it, I should have seen it. I should have known!"

Tears clawed at his throat, warring with the rage in his heart. He'd missed it because it wasn't any of the normal mortal illnesses. It wasn't cancer or HIV or tuberculosis. It wasn't even the massive amounts of snake venom pouring through Seth's veins, although that certainly wasn't helping. It was something humans didn't even have a name for. Something buried in Seth's supernatural parentage, born of the cancer and disease and pain he'd absorbed through the years. It was something that even Abaddon couldn't cure.

"It's okay," Seth whispered. He tried to reach up, to put his fingers against Abaddon's cheeks, but he didn't have the strength. His hand fell limp at his side. "We're all dying. 'Yea, though I walk through the valley of the shadow of death—'"

"Stop it! Goddamn it, no bible verses! Don't make excuses for Him." Because what kind of God would allow this to happen? "You have to stop healing people. You have to stop letting the snakes come. You have to—"

"You're scaring them, Abaddon."

"Wh-what?"

He'd been so focused on Seth he hadn't noticed the crowd gathered around them. He hadn't heard their frightened murmurs. Zed suddenly appeared at his side. He knelt and reached for Seth. Abaddon instinctively gripped Seth tighter, pulling him out of Zed's reach. "Get away from him!"

"Let him go," Zed growled back. "This isn't your place."

"It's okay," Seth said. Abaddon wasn't sure which one of them he was addressing. "It's okay."

"He's all right, folks!" Thaddeus said, raising his voice above the din of the crowd. "The Lord's touch is a powerful thing. It often leaves my brother exhausted, but never fear! He has the blessings of the almighty savior! Can I get a 'hallelujah'?"

A few people echoed him. "Hallelujah!" It sounded more like a question than an exclamation.

"Just give him some air, now. Let him breathe. Brother Zed and Brother Abbadon will have him sorted out in no time. The best thing we can do for him is to raise our voices in praise!"

Abaddon hated the words, but he had to appreciate Thaddeus's efficiency. The crowd backed up. The band began playing, the choir singing "How Great Thou Art", and Thaddeus's voice rose above it all, leading them in song.

Zed edged closer, grabbing Seth's arm as if he intended to physically wrench the boy from Abaddon's embrace. "You have become too familiar, Brother Abaddon. Let him go and stand aside."

"It's okay," Seth said again, and this time, his blind eyes met Abaddon's gaze. This time, his fingers found Abaddon's cheek. "I'll be all right. Zed knows what to do. I'm not dying yet, I promise."

It was true. Already, Seth's strength was returning, his soul fading to its normal brilliance. Color was slowly returning to his cheeks. His kidney's were damaged, and his liver too, but neither of those things were the real problem. The real problem lay buried in his inhuman genes.

Abaddon loosened his grip, his mind a jumble, sifting through his limited options. He barely noticed as Zed pulled Seth from his arms.

There wasn't much time.

And he had the entire bureaucracy of Hell to deal with.

Chapter Eight
Ice Cream So Bad, It's (Not) a Sin

Hours in Hell were hard to track, and without the sun dancing slowly across the sky, it was hard to tell one day from the next. The office was busy when Abaddon arrived, even though it felt to him like the middle of the night. He was relieved to find Baphomet still at his desk, folding forms. The chair Abaddon had stolen from a nearby cubicle on his last visit was still next to Baphomet's desk, and Abaddon sank gratefully into it, wondering where to begin.

"You look like hell."

"Is that supposed to be funny?" Abaddon scrubbed his fingers through his hair and eyed the stack of papers on Baphomet's desk. "Shouldn't you be done with these?"

"You have any idea how long it takes to fold a hundred and fifty million forms?"

Abaddon winced, thinking how his desk must look by now. It was possible it was completely buried under paperwork. He'd have to deal with it eventually, but not yet. "I need your help."

"Uh-uh. No way." Baphomet stuffed a form into another envelope. "Helping anybody in Hell is against the rules. You know that."

"You've helped me before."

"You can't prove that."

"I need to know if there's a way to file for an extension."

"Are you crazy? You're already on probation! Now you want an extension too?"

"Is it possible?"

Baphomet shook his head, but the faraway look in his eyes told Abaddon that he was thinking about it. "Well, there are dispensations for special circumstances, like people who agree to sign over their souls once certain things are in place. It's like they give you a promise ring rather than an actual engagement ring, even though everybody knows they mean the same thing. There are also cases where the mortal agrees to give his soul, but the devil's part of the agreement takes extra time to fulfill. You'd have to fill out a 10-382, and a 12-685, and a 13-387, and—"

"There's more." Abaddon glanced around, making sure nobody was listening. The closest devil was two cubicles away at the copier that had come to Hell courtesy of 1985. His hands and chest were covered in toner as he cursed and pounded on the machine. He wasn't paying Abbaddon and Baphomet a bit of attention. Abaddon turned back to Baphomet and leaned closer. "Anybody who loses their soul to one of us ends up here, right?"

Baphomet lowered the envelope he'd been about to lick. "Right."

"But the Soul Acquisition Department must be thirty floors at least, and each of them several miles worth of cubicles, right?"

"I don't like where this is going."

"Is there any way to find a specific person once they arrive? Or any way to make sure they're stationed nearby once they do? I mean, it'd take me forever to find him going cubicle to cubicle, especially when we all work different hours, but if there's a way to know where he'll be—"

"Abaddon, stop." Baphomet set his envelope aside and leaned closer. "This is crazy. You need to forget about this kid, okay? Forget about his perfect soul and find somebody else."

"I can't."

"You're obsessed."

"I know!" Baphomet was right. At this point, it might be wiser to settle for a few pedestrian souls, but he couldn't stand the thought of being without Seth. And now, maybe he wouldn't have to. "Just answer me! I don't have much time!"

Baphomet sighed and leaned back in his chair. "I swear, you're the lousiest devil I've ever met." He pinched the bridge of his nose. "Yes, there's a way to file for assignment to a nearby station, but not for the reasons you're thinking. This is Hell, not kindergarten. They don't care that you've suddenly decided you want a new pet—"

"It isn't like that!"

"They only care if you have some kind of grudge, like a mortal who pissed you off, and you want to be able to torture them over time. You'll have to put on a good show to convince them that you hate him. And one more thing you haven't thought of."

"What's that?"

"He won't even know you once he crosses over. He'll have forgotten everything about you."

Talk about being sucker-punched by the fine print. Abaddon sat back, reeling. He put his hands to his head, fighting a sudden blackness that seemed to cloud his vision. How could he have forgotten about that? Just as he didn't remember any of his mortal life, Seth wouldn't remember him. The knowledge bent him in half, and he found himself clutching his stomach, staring at the floor, gasping for breath. "I think I'm going to be sick."

"Abaddon, you're off the deep end, man. What's going on?"

Abaddon shook his head, fighting tears. "I thought if I could bring him here— If I could have him nearby—"

He felt Baphomet's hand on his shoulder. "If you care about him so much, leave him where he is. Visit him on the mortal plane whenever you can. You wouldn't be the first devil to do it."

"He's dying." He put a hand over his face. He was relieved to find that his eyes were dry. He sat up again, trying to reclaim his focus. "It's part of why he burns so bright. It's part of what makes him such a perfect catch."

"Ah. So if he's going to die anyway—"

"I thought if I could at least have him nearby…" He wasn't ready to give up yet. "There must be a way, and you know the loopholes better than anyone."

Baphomet put his chin in his hand, thinking, and Abaddon waited. He didn't have much faith in God these days, but he had faith in his friend. And sure enough, a moment later, Baphomet's eyes went wide.

"Wait a minute!" He opened a desk drawer and pulled out a binder with a four-inch spine. Rules and Regulations of the Department of Soul Acquisitions. He began flipping through pages. "Maybe…"

In the end, it would be nearly two dozen forms to file, all in triplicate, at three different offices: a DMV in Phoenix, another in Detroit, and a social security office in New Jersey.

"How long will it take?" Abaddon asked, anxious for the first time ever to begin filling out paperwork.

Baphomet scratched his chin, considering. "On your own? A couple of weeks. But with my help?" He smiled. "I think we can wrap it up in about five mortal days. That puts you over your deadline, so we'll have to file for the extension first."

Relief flooded through him. "You'd do that for me?"

"Sure. I'm sick of licking envelopes anyway. I'll go get the forms and meet you back at your desk." He stood and raised his voice. "Now get away from me, you rotten, no-good bastard! I hope you burn in the Lake of Fire for an eternity!"

Abaddon shouted a few curses of his own on his way back to his desk, just for good measure, but in his heart, he rejoiced.

There was hope after all.

He just needed a few extra days.

Half an hour later, he and Baphomet settled at adjacent desks and got to work.

There were forms asking for an extension of his deadline, forms promising delivery of a spectacular soul under special circumstances, forms to assign a newly acquired soul to a select region of the department in order to prolong the former mortal's torment, forms that stated only that other forms had been filed, and finally, forms to allow Seth to retain his memory after crossing into Hell. The latter required that Seth have personal knowledge that could assist him in soul acquisition. The revival provided that—a fresh crop of devout, trusting mortals who could theoretically be convinced to give their soul to Seth, even after he became a devil. Seth would never do such a thing, of course, but they'd deal with that later. A bit more paperwork down the road seemed like a small price to pay to keep Seth nearby.

But once the paperwork was filed, Abaddon had no way out. No amount of regular mortal souls could save him now. He'd have three days to secure Seth's soul, or be damned to some lower level of Hell. It was the Department's version of going double-or-nothing with the boss. If he didn't return with Seth, he'd be demoted, no explanations, apologies or excuses. There was no back-up plan. No second chances.

Everything depended on Seth.

Of course he'd be well and truly screwed if Seth died before he got everything in place, so he made a quick stop on his way to Detroit at the campground in Alabama.

It was deserted.

"Satan's tits!" Abaddon kicked at the dirt. "Where the fuck did they go?" He spun in a circle, looking around, as if he might have somehow missed a giant revival tent and the few dozen trailers, semis, and trucks that went with it. But no. There was no sign of Seth.

It was harder to search in mortal form, so he withdrew into the abyss and cast his mental web wide. They only had a ten to twelve hour jump on him, but which direction would they have gone? He was impatient, annoyed at having one more thing to take up his time, desperate to find Seth and know for sure that he was safe. It took five precious hours of searching, but finally, his mind snagged on the unmistakable brilliance of Seth's soul at a campground in Georgia. He nearly wept with relief.

The Rainbow Revival camp was dark and quiet. No revival tonight, after a day of traveling. He hesitated, his body still hidden in the abyss, his consciousness outside of Seth's trailer. He could easily peer inside, if he wanted to. He'd never spied on Seth before, and he was reluctant to do so now, but his only other options were to knock on Seth's door, possibly waking any light sleepers in the vicinity in the process, or wait until morning for Seth to appear.

He sincerely hated both options.

He cast a cautious feeler into the trailer—not quite looking, but *feeling.*

Seth was definitely inside.

Definitely asleep.

Abaddon took a deep breath and manifested in the confines of the trailer.

He'd never been in Seth's living space before. It was like most travel trailers: a tiny kitchen, with a two-burner stove, a sink, and a miniature fridge on one side, and a table between bench seats on the other. Beyond that was a narrow door that probably led to the bathroom, and a sleeping area at the back. It was an older trailer, with accents in orange and avocado green. The tabletop had started out yellow, but was now worn mostly white. A coffee cup, a fork, and a single plate sat in the drying rack. Everything else was clean and uncluttered. If Seth had ever had photos, he'd taken them down since losing his sight. A bible was the only thing visible, its cover tattered, and Abaddon stopped to wonder about that. Seth couldn't read it. Did he still find comfort in its pages?

Abaddon ran his finger over the frayed book. There was no shock from touching the supposed word of God. No lightning came to strike him down.

"Abaddon?"

He jumped, turning to find Seth in the doorway that led to the tiny space that served as a bedroom. There was no scarf around his neck. He wore only flannel pajama pants— red with a black moose print—and a faded T-shirt that had probably once been green. It was inside out, but Abaddon could see the faint outline of Snoopy's friend Woodstock through the fabric. The effect was somehow both adorable and sexy as hell.

Abaddon cleared his throat. "I didn't mean to wake you."

"I know."

Abaddon scratched his neck, thinking. He was pretty sure he hadn't made any noise. "How did you know I was here?"

"I'm not sure, to be honest. I just did." Seth settled against the doorframe, tilting his head against it. At that moment, he was definitely leaning more toward adorable in Abaddon's mind.

"I didn't think you'd pack up and go so quickly."

"We always leave after an event."

"You mean after you heal somebody?"

"Thaddeus and Zed don't want the media finding out. They worry people will show up with cameras. They don't want it to become a spectacle."

Abaddon almost laughed. Most revivalists lived for spectacle, but he thought better of Thaddeus and Zed for their reluctance to exploit Seth's ability.

"I suppose that makes sense." He looked Seth up and down, moving closer. He still looked tired. The bites on his neck were swollen and red. "Are you all right?"

"I'm fine." Seth smiled, and the scales tipped a bit toward sexy. "I'm glad you're here."

Abaddon reached for Seth's hand, but stopped short. They were in such tight quarters, and in Seth's personal space too. Everything felt more intimate. "I hated to leave when I did."

"It's okay. I was in good hands. Zed knows what to do."

"How long have you known?"

"That I could heal people? Since the first time the snakes came. I must have been nine or ten."

"No. I mean, how long have you known that you're dying?"

"Oh, that." How could he sound so casual about it? How could he talk so easily about something that filled Abaddon with equal measures of dread and hope? "Since I was eighteen. I think I suspected before that, but that was when I truly understood what it cost me to heal them."

"And yet, you keep doing it." Seth didn't answer except to duck his head, and Abaddon's grief grew. "That's why you wanted to leave when you were eighteen? You knew you were running out of time?"

Seth nodded, a short, uncomfortable gesture. "That was part of it, yes. I thought it'd give me a bit longer. But mostly..." He bit his lip, his eyes settling somewhere near Abaddon's face. "Mostly I just wanted to do more before I died. To see more, you know? I wanted a chance to meet somebody. I wanted..."

He stopped, his cheeks flushing pink. This time, Abaddon took his hand. "You wanted a chance to fall in love."

Tears brimmed in Seth's eyes. "Yes." He ducked his head, but he couldn't stop the flood of emotion that surged through him. Abaddon's supernatural senses detected a truckload of embarrassment, but underneath it was an undercurrent of gratefulness that took Abaddon's breath away. After everything that had happened, Seth felt he'd been granted his greatest wish.

He'd been given a chance to fall in love, after all.

Abaddon steeled closer. His fingers shook as he wiped Seth's tears away. "You knew I wouldn't stop looking until I found you."

"I hoped." Seth's smile was sweet and hesitant. "You once told me that my soul is like a beacon to you. Like a lighthouse."

Abaddon had to force himself to speak around the lump in his throat. "You are my guiding star."

"I don't know if it worked, but..." He bit his lip, looking almost flirtatious, although he'd probably never intentionally flirted with anybody in his life. "I tried to shine extra bright for you."

Abaddon's heart clenched, and he pulled Seth into his arms and held him tight. He was overwhelmed as always by the power of Seth's soul and the brightness of his heart, but for the first time ever, those took a backseat to his own feelings. He barely knew Seth, but he loved him with a fierceness that terrified him. He wanted Seth to live forever, but he also longed for the day he could take him home. Maybe Seth didn't belong in Hell, but at least they'd be together. At least he'd still be able to touch him, and to see him. Was that so terrible of a thing to want?

Seth fit perfectly against him, his arms around Abaddon's waist, his face tucked into Abaddon's neck, his warm breath tickling the sensitive place just below Abaddon's ear, and even the sudden surge of arousal he felt couldn't wash away the grief in his heart.

How in the world could he love Seth so much? And after finally realizing it, how could he bear to let him go?

"Abaddon, you're shaking. Are you okay?"

"I'm fine," Abaddon lied, turning to kiss Seth's temple. "I'm fine." He pulled back a bit so he could look into Seth's trusting face. Should he tell him now what he planned? He debated, but decided it was better to wait until everything was in place.

Seth shifted against him, suddenly averting his eyes, and Abaddon felt the gentle nudge of flesh as Seth began to grow hard inside his pajama pants. Abaddon had to bite his lip to keep from moaning. He had to brace himself to keep from kissing Seth again and angling him toward the bed, but one glance at Seth's face stilled him. Seth was blushing furiously, trying to pull away in the narrow confines of the trailer, beyond embarrassed at what was happening. Abaddon took a deep breath and let him go. He let Seth turn away and rest his face against the doorframe.

"Seth…" He wanted to say: "There's no reason to be embarrassed." He wanted to say: "It's natural." He wanted to say: "I know exactly how you feel. I want you even more than you want me." But he had a feeling Seth already knew all of those things.

Still, being a virgin as he undoubtedly was, it took Seth a minute to find his voice again.

"I'm sorry."

"There's no reason to be." He touched Seth's hair, but didn't allow himself any more contact than that. "You don't have to apologize to me for anything."

Seth kept his face averted, but Abaddon heard his soft exhale as he smiled. "Then thank you for not laughing at me."

No, he couldn't laugh at him for this, but he regretted having to let him go. He wanted nothing more than to hold him again, but he didn't want to make things more difficult than they needed to be.

Besides, he was running out of time.

He took Seth's hand and steered him to the kitchen table. And although it was hard in such tight quarters, he managed to kneel at Seth's feet, their clasped hands resting on Seth's knees. "I need to ask you something."

"Okay."

"Do you know how much time…?" Jesus, what kind of way was that to begin?

"How long before I die, you mean?"

"Yes."

"Not exactly. I know it won't be long now." Seth's voice got quieter as he spoke. "A week or two, I think. Why?"

"I have something I need to do. I'll be gone a few days. I didn't want you to worry, and I didn't want—" He stopped, choking on the words.

"You didn't want to come back and find out I was already gone." Abaddon winced, but Seth only smiled. "We haven't had time to do any advertising or anything here. That means we won't host a revival for several more days at least."

No revival meant no snakes.

No snakes meant no healing.

And no healing meant a little more time.

"I promise you, I'll be back. I think it'll be three or four days at the most."

"Okay." Seth pulled one of his hands free and covered Abaddon's, like the game children played, pulling their hand from the bottom of the stack to place it on top. "I'll miss you, but I understand."

"I'll come back."

"You've already said that, and I have no reason to doubt you. You've never lied to me, as far as I know." He smiled, cocking his head. "Except now that I think about it, you do still owe me ice cream."

Abaddon laughed, rocking back on his heels. "What flavor?"

Seth's brow wrinkled in puzzlement. "Any flavor?"

"You name it."

Seth put one finger on his chin as he thought. "Pistachio. With caramel swirl, and chocolate chips."

"That's an absolute travesty. All the flavors in the world, and you pick pistachio? It's an insult to ice cream everywhere."

"Are you saying you can't do it?"

Abaddon laughed at the challenge. "Bowl or cone?"

"Cone."

"Cake, waffle, or sugar?"

"Sugar."

"You got it."

It was easy to pull it from the abyss. A slight bending of the rules maybe, but with all that paperwork in Hell, one little ice cream cone wouldn't be missed. He placed it in Seth's hand. Such a simple gesture, but it made his heart ache, and before he could think worse of it, he put his other hand behind Seth's neck and drew him into a kiss.

A careful kiss, soft and gentle. Just enough to taste Seth's sweetness, to hear Seth's breath catch in his throat, to feel the way Seth thrilled at his touch.

If he didn't leave now, he never would.

"I'll be back as soon as I can."

"I know."

He stood, backing up, wanting to put distance between them before he dove into the abyss. But before he could bring himself to leave, Seth spoke.

"Abaddon?"

"Yes?"

"Do you think eating ice cream from Hell is a sin?"

Abaddon laughed. "Not when it's pistachio."

DMVs were bad enough for mortals, but after taking the little number from the machine and sitting down to wait their turn, mortals never noticed that certain numbers were never called. Even after all the humans had gone and the doors had been locked, a dozen devils sat slumped in plastic chairs, waiting. When that was done, it was on to the next office, where he stood in line for twenty-two hours before being allowed to plead his case to some upper-crust devil with garlic breath. Four days after handing Seth pistachio ice cream, Abaddon returned to his cubicle in

Hell. He couldn't quite find his desk under the mountain of memos, but he found a note taped to the wall.

Abaddon: It's done. You are an oozing mole on Satan's right butt cheek. I hope you get biopsied.
—B

Abaddon breathed a sigh of relief. His legs and back ached. His head was pounding, his eyes dry and burning, but at least it hadn't been for nothing.

He needed to rest, but he wanted to be sure Seth was safe first. A quick peek at the Rainbow Revival campground showed him it was the dead of night in Georgia. Seth was sound asleep in his bed. His sweet brilliance ebbed and flowed with his even breaths. Abaddon hesitated, feeling like everything in the world would be made right if he could only climb into bed next to Seth and hold him close, but he resisted. He was already exhausted, and if he managed to get into Seth's bed—something he wouldn't be able to do without resorting to methods he was no longer willing to use—he sure as hell wouldn't want to sleep.

He took the subway back to his tenement, swaying on his feet as he hung from the hand strap. He had to lean against the wall as he climbed the stairs to his room. And finally, he fell into the relative comfort of his own bed.

At some point in the not-too-distant future, he'd have Seth here with him in Hell. Sirens blared and roosters crowed. Abaddon listened to the clamor, picturing Seth in some distant tenement. He imagined Seth's dismay at the never-ending din. His horror at having to trick mortals out of their soul. His sadness when he learned music didn't exist in Hell.

Abaddon rubbed his hand over his pilled, scratchy sheets and imagined introducing Seth to the true glory of sin in the gloomy stink of his apartment, so far from God that even somebody as devout of Seth was bound to lose his faith.

He imagined Seth without his soul.

It was a long time before Abaddon slept.

Chapter Nine
Sift Like What?

It was just after lunch by the time Abaddon made it back to the Rainbow Revival. Preparations were in full swing. He spotted Seth in the center of camp, surrounded by some of his friends, but he held back, trying to rein in his demonic senses, trying not to focus on the perfection of Seth's soul.

It was an impossible task. Now that he was attuned to it, he couldn't ignore it, even if he wanted to.

If he faced Seth now, he'd either kiss him or burst into tears, and neither possibility begged an audience. Instead, he hid in Seth's empty trailer. He sat at the tiny kitchen table with his head in his hands, staring at Seth's ratty old bible, almost wishing he could find comfort there.

Anywhere, really.

Finally, the door opened and Seth came in.

"Abaddon?"

Abaddon found it harder than usual to make his throat work. "Yes. I'm here."

Seth smiled, leaning back against the two-burner stove. "Zed told me you were waiting."

"Zed?" How in the world had he known? That old man was proving to be more trouble every day.

"You did it, then? Whatever it was you had to do?"

Abaddon stood, wanting to move closer. Wanting more than anything to pull Seth into his arms. "I did."

Seth ducked his head, scuffing his toe against the tile floor in embarrassment. "I missed you."

He looked so young at that moment—younger even than his mere twenty-two years—and Abaddon's self-loathing grew. "I need to tell you something." And yet, it was so hard to make himself say the words. He reached for Seth, but stopped short. He settled instead for taking Seth's hands—the right one perfectly soft and supple, the left with heavy calluses on the fingertips from guitar and fiddle strings. "I went back to Hell for a reason. I was looking for a way— Well, I found a way—" He choked, seeing in his mind again the image of Seth stuck in Hell. "Jesus, this shouldn't be so hard."

Seth squeezed his fingers. "Tell me."

Abaddon took a deep breath. "I found a way we can be together." But his throat was tight. It was hard to make the words come out. "After…"

"After I'm dead?"

Abaddon jerked his head in a nod, realizing too late the gesture was lost on Seth. "Yes."

"Does it involve me giving you my soul?"

Abaddon couldn't stand to look in those blind, trusting eyes. "Yes."

"Could you…could you heal me, in exchange for my soul?"

"I don't know. If you were human, yes. But since you're not—"

"What? What do you mean?"

Whether Seth had pulled him closer, or vice versa, Abaddon didn't know, but what had started out as a foot or two of empty space between them was now mere inches. Abaddon fought to keep his mind focused. "You're different, Seth. That's part of why you burn so bright. You're extraordinary. You're—"

"What if I just gave you my soul, asking nothing in return? Would you take it?"

Abaddon winced. "I'd have to." He'd never hated himself so much. "But don't. Please. It's not right."

"Isn't that what you want? For us to be together?"

"It is." It was all he could do to keep his tears at bay. "It is, but Seth—"

"It's okay." Seth smiled up at him, although it was the saddest smile Abaddon had ever seen. "I won't do it anyway. I won't forsake my soul, Abaddon. Not even for you."

"Good." Abaddon breathed a sigh of relief, not even bothering to wonder that he felt it at all. This meant he was doomed, but he hardly cared. "That's as it should be. I want you more than anything, but you don't belong with me." He kissed Seth's forehead, reveling in the sweetness that seemed to pour from Seth's skin. He let his lips play over Seth's beautiful, blind eyes. His heart pounded as he moved to Seth's mouth, kissing him at last, but trying not to push. Trying not to dive too deep, even though he was desperate to do just that. Seth shifted his weight, moving closer, letting their bodies meet in a way that made Abaddon's entire body thrum with arousal.

"Abaddon?" His voice was barely a whisper, his lips brushing Abaddon's as he spoke.

"Yes."

"I've been thinking a lot since that last time you were here."

"And?"

"My soul may belong to God." He took Abaddon's hand and guided it to the soft bulge between his legs. "But all the rest of me belongs to you."

How could something be both so right and so wrong? How could it make him feel so much joy and so much grief? "No." Abaddon ducked his head into Seth's hair, moaning as Seth's flesh began to harden beneath his fingers. "No, you don't want to do this."

"I've never wanted anything as much as I want this."

"It's wrong."

"I've never known the touch of a woman, or of a man."

"Seth, please—"

"And I think maybe I'd like to."

"Oh, hell's bells, don't tempt me like this. You have no idea what you're doing to me."

But Seth's grip on Abaddon's hand didn't ease. His erection warmed Abaddon's palm, and Seth pushed, guiding Abaddon's hand into a caress. "I'm dying."

"I know," Abaddon choked, trying to stop the slow movement of his hand and failing completely. "But that doesn't mean you should throw it all away."

"I'm not."

"But—"

"I've lived righteously for twenty-two years, and I won't live to see twenty-three. I want…" He took a deep, shaking breath, and when he spoke again, his voice was barely a whisper. "I want to know what it's like to share myself with somebody I love. And if God is as charitable as I believe, He'll forgive me that one simple sin."

"But not with me! Don't you see how wrong it is? 'Seth, oh Seth, behold, Satan doth desire to have you. He longs to possess you, to own you, that he may sift you as wheat.'"

Seth laughed. "That's not quite how it goes."

"Close enough."

Seth's smile was as pure and sweet and gorgeous as the sunrise. "So sift me already, you damned fool."

And he pulled Abaddon into a kiss.

Some part of his brain wanted to resist, but that small voice was drowned out by everything else. Seth was bright and perfect and pure, the glorious sweetness of his soul filling Abaddon's senses, making him oblivious to everything but his desire. He moved his hand, just barely, brushing his thumb up the length of Seth's erection through his jeans. Seth shivered and gasped in response, clinging to him.

"Yes," he breathed.

And the beast Abaddon had been fighting since that very first night reared up in his heart and in his mind, finally tearing free of its constraints. God help him, but he wanted Seth in a way that was entirely inhuman, and he was tired of fighting it. He kissed Seth harder, growling as his need became more urgent, tugging at his clothes, ripping Seth's shirt in his urgency as he pushed him toward the bed. He had no thought of reining in that passion. He fumbled with the buttons of his jeans and Seth helped, pushing them impatiently down, over Abaddon's hips, both of them gasping and rushing, reckless and desperate, until they fell at last naked onto the sheets. Seth's flesh was cool to the touch, but his essence was hot as the sun, his soul burning like cinnamon candy on Abaddon's tongue, and he strained, every inch of him taut and trembling with a need he hadn't felt in all his years as a devil. There was too much—too much longing and too much pent-up hunger—and when Seth's soft fingers closed around his cock, Abaddon cried out. The brightness flared, blinding him, coursing through him, shooting from his loins in achingly satisfying bursts until he collapsed, panting and shaking. It was so new and alien and unbelievable that it took him a minute to realize what had happened.

"Wow," Seth said quietly. "I figured I'd be the one with that problem."

"Shit! I'm sorry! That wasn't supposed to happen."

Seth laughed, guiding Abaddon's lips to his. "I don't mind."

But Abaddon had never felt like a bigger ass. Seth was throwing away a lifetime of sinless living for one roll in the hay, and Abaddon had blown it.

Literally.

"This was supposed to be for you!"

"No. It was supposed to be for us. And we have plenty of time."

Yes, they did. And now that Abaddon's urgency had been purged in the most embarrassing way possible, he saw that maybe it was for the best. Seth deserved something more than a rushed, frantic one-off, and if he was going to arrive at Heaven's gates with only one sin on his ledger, well...

Might as well make it count.

Abaddon used Seth's ruined shirt to clean him off, kissing him as he did. And when that was done, he focused on teasing Seth's flesh with fingers and lips and tongue, searching for the places that elicited the best response.

They weren't hard to find, because the snakes had found them first. The tiny, round scars in perfect sets of two were like breadcrumbs on the trail. Abaddon followed them down Seth's body, from the crook of his neck to his smooth, flat belly; and finally, to the tender flesh on the insides of his thighs. Abaddon lapped at those scars, tasting cotton candy and cinnamon, kissing with his lips, nipping with his teeth, and Seth went wild, panting and moaning, biting his lip to stifle his cries lest somebody hear him through the trailer's thin walls.

Abaddon moved away from the scars once to trace his tongue up Seth's erection, but Seth pushed him back to his thighs, back to those scars, whimpering as Abbadon locked his mouth there and used his hand instead, rubbing his thumb gently up Seth's length. A few featherlight strokes was all it took to trigger Seth's climax.

When it was over, Seth pulled Abaddon up so they were face-to-face. He seemed oblivious to the mess between them. Abaddon expected to see wonder, or amazement, or at least a smile. But instead, Seth looked afraid.

"Tell me you'll stay," he whispered. "Tell me this isn't the end."

Whether he meant the end of their sexual encounter or the end of his life or the end of their relationship, Abaddon didn't know. It didn't matter.

"I'm not going anywhere."

"Tell me you love me."

They'd only known each other two weeks. Maybe it was foolish, but Abaddon didn't hesitate. "You know I do."

Seth made a sound that was almost a sob, and for a minute, Abaddon just held him, stroking his hair, making soothing sounds until Seth quieted. Even then, he only let him go because the mess between them was becoming difficult to ignore.

"I didn't mean to turn into an emotional basket case," Seth said as they untangled their limbs.

"I think you're entitled."

They cleaned up again, then settled back in the bed, this time pulling the covers over them. Seth nestled into Abaddon's arms, rubbing his hand over Abaddon's chest, trailing his fingers lightly through his chest hair. He followed it down to Abaddon's navel, then an inch or two past that before stopping, ducking his head against Abaddon's chest in a way that told Abaddon he was blushing.

It was kind of adorable, really, how he was still shy about going any lower.

They dozed for a while, sated and comfortable, but the temptation of skin against skin was too great. At some point, their warmth once again became fire. Soft kisses and gentle caresses became more urgent.

"Will you do something for me?" Seth asked, breathless. Abaddon could tell by his voice it was something he was unsure of. "If I asked it, would you—"

"Anything." Abaddon kissed him, putting the weight of his promise into that simple gesture. "Absolutely anything. Just name it."

Seth smiled. And then…

Seth didn't actually ask anything. Instead, he pushed Abaddon gently down, under the sheets.

"Is that all?" Abaddon asked, laughing.

But Seth was already lost again, gasping, straining toward him. "Please."

His intent was clear, and Abaddon gladly obliged him. He teased his tongue around the head of Seth's cock before swallowing him whole. He tucked his hands underneath Seth's soft backside, urging him in deeper. Seth didn't need guidance for long. After only a few thrusts, he was the one moving, holding Abaddon's head, pushing with his hips, making the most beautiful, erotic sounds Abaddon had ever heard. He was amazed how even now, engaged in one of the most carnal sins in the book, Seth's perfect, blinding brilliance didn't wane. It glowed from his eyes. It emanated from his pores and pulsed through his loins. It filled the tiny room, rippling over them, so vivid and real that Abaddon was sure it must be blazing from the windows of the trailer, a beacon for all to see. Even with Seth panting in pleasure, whimpering as he thrust deeper into Abaddon's throat, that purity wasn't diminished.

Abaddon gripped Seth tighter, lost in the moment, blind and dumb and utterly powerless. And when Seth finally came, it was the most delicious thing Abaddon had ever tasted, like orange honey and cinnamon heart candy, and Seth's bright laughter felt like a cold spring rain, washing him clean, even as Abaddon spent himself against the sheets.

"Oh, man," Seth said, breathless. "That was almost worth going to Hell for."

Abaddon wanted to laugh. He tried, but the mental image of Seth stuck in Hell rose up harsh and angry in his mind. He imagined again Seth's brilliance slowly fading away to nothing in a distant cubicle, and his laughter came out a bitter sob.

Seth deserved better than Hell.

Seth's hand moved on his head like a blessing. "'What mean ye to weep and to break mine heart? For I am ready not to be bound only, but also to die at Jerusalem for the name of the Lord Jesus.'"

Abaddon laid his forehead against Seth's soft belly, letting his tears fall on the many scars left by the snakes. Outside, people laughed as they prepared for the revival. Canvas slapped in the wind. "I've never hated God as much as I do right now."

Seth sat up suddenly, forcing Abaddon to do the same. He reached for Abaddon, brushing his fingers down Abaddon's cheek. "Don't. Please. Not on my account, Abaddon. I couldn't bear it."

"You're the one who should be angry. It amazes me that you can be so calm."

"I'm not, though. I'm terrified. I know I shouldn't be. My faith tells me I'm going to a wondrous place and that there's nothing to fear, but I've never been so scared in my life."

"That's normal. It's…" Abaddon almost choked. "It's human." But thinking about Seth's easy acceptance of what was coming gave Abaddon a new idea. Why hadn't he thought of it before? "What if we left?"

"Left the revival, you mean?"

"We could take your truck and your trailer and just drive. We could go anywhere. I could take you to the Grand Canyon. I could give you your sight for a minute, at least. I could let you feel the wind rushing up the canyon wall onto your face. Isn't that what you want?"

Seth gave him a soft, sad smile. He took Abaddon's hand, holding it between both of his. "Is it so easy to escape Hell?"

Abaddon's heart clenched. Tears filled his eyes, and he covered them with his free hand. "No. You're my only chance now. If I come back without you…"

Seth squeezed his fingers. "What? What happens?"

Abaddon shook his head. He wasn't going to burden Seth with the truth. The last thing he wanted was for Seth to feel guilty because some worthless devil got sent to a deeper level of Hell. "I'll be heartbroken. That's all. I just thought…" What? What in the world had he been thinking, asking Seth to run away with him, as if that would solve everything? "I wouldn't be able to go with you, but I could at least give you your sight." He'd pay for it later, and he'd never see Seth again, but wouldn't it be worth it? "You'd at least have enough time to go there yourself. To see a few of the places on your list."

But Seth was already shaking his head. "I can't run away from this. I tried once, and I went blind. And I know you'll tell me it was just bad luck and not God sending me a message, but what if you're wrong? Yes, I could run away, and it might buy me an extra day or an extra week, but at what cost?" He put his fingers against Abaddon's cheek and leaned close, as if he could look into Abaddon's eyes. "I have weighed my transgressions, Abaddon. I know where I stand. Now, I must follow Christ's example and face my death—"

"You're not Him!"

"I know. I would never make such a presumptuous claim. But the message is clear. I must stand strong in the face of adversity, armed with nothing but the promise of God's love. I could give you half a dozen other examples from the bible—"

"I don't want to hear them!"

Seth laughed, brushing his thumb over Abaddon's lips. "I know you don't. I know it makes you crazy when I start spouting bible verses."

"Only when it's to justify something stupid!"

Seth jerked his hands away, his face falling into the same hurt, uncomprehending look a puppy gave his master after being kicked. Abaddon would have preferred a knife in his chest to seeing that wounded expression on Seth's face.

"Please don't call me stupid. This is all I have. I have my faith in God, and I have you. Please don't try to take one of them away."

Abaddon groaned. He really was the world's biggest jerk. "I'm sorry." He took Seth's hands and leaned over to place his forehead on them. "You're right. I'm being selfish, and I'm sorry, but I can't help it. I wish I could accept it as easily as you, but it makes me so angry."

"I know." Seth placed his other hand on the back of Abaddon's head, ruffling his fingers through his hair. "But you will accept it. I want you to promise me, Abaddon. I want you to promise that when the time comes, you won't try to stop it. I want you to promise me that you'll let me face the serpents, and heal the sick, regardless of the cost. I need you to promise that you'll be there at the very end, but that you won't interfere in the process."

Abaddon's breath hitched. He couldn't hold back the tears that filled his eyes. He hated this plan. He hated it with every devilish fiber of his being. He hated it more than he hated God. More than he hated Hell.

But it wasn't about him.

"I promise," he choked. "Oh God, I promise."

"Thank you."

Abaddon wept.

Chapter Ten
Everybody Loves a Bad Boy

Not much later, somebody knocked on the trailer door. Abaddon prepared to dive into the abyss, but whoever it was didn't come in. They just yelled through the door, "Time to start, Seth!"

"I'll be right there!"

Seth moved easily about his small bedroom despite his blindness, taking out khaki slacks and a clean, white dress shirt. Socks and shoes came next, then finally, a blue silk scarf, which he wrapped around his neck to cover the many scars. And all the while, Abaddon sat at the tiny table in Seth's trailer with his head in his hands, hating Thaddeus and Zed and the Rainbow Revivalists and God and Hell in equal measures.

Seth laid his hand on Abaddon's bowed head. After finally making love, the brilliant power of Seth's soul hadn't changed, but its effect on Abaddon had. Instead of burning hunger, he felt only love and overwhelming grief.

"I wish I could take this pain from you, the way I can for the sick."

"No." Abaddon shook his head. "I would never ask that of you. I'd rather bear it myself than burden you with it."

Seth laughed. "You're a terrible devil, you know. You miss all kinds of great chances to be evil."

Yes, he was a terrible devil. It was the reason he'd missed his quota in the first place. And now, he'd not only failed to secure Seth's soul, he'd also doomed himself to an eternity without him. But time was short, and Seth needed him to be strong.

He wiped his eyes and stood. He pulled Seth into his arms. He kissed him, savoring that wonderful sweetness. He pulled back to look into Seth's eyes.

"I love you. No matter what happens, I want you to know that."

Seth's brow wrinkled. "I do." He frowned. "Abaddon, you're scaring me. I feel like there's something you're not telling me."

Once again, Abaddon had to wonder if the soul sense went both ways. "I told you I'd be here until the end, but it may not be possible."

"What? But you promised."

"I know, but it's a promise I may have to break."

"No! You can't do that to me. You said—"

"I'll try, Seth, but there's a chance I'll be gone in a couple of days—"

"You promised!"

He pushed at Abaddon, trying to get away, and Abaddon grabbed his arms, shaking him a bit in his urgency to say it all. "I know! And I'll do everything I can to keep that promise, but once they figure out what I've done…" Once his time was up, there'd be no appeal. "If Hell takes me away, I won't be able to come back no matter how much I'll want to. But I want you to know that I'll do everything I can. I want you to believe me when I say that I've never cared about anyone the way I care about you."

Seth blinked, his cheeks paler than usual. "But, I need you. If you're not here…" He shook his head, his focus shifting to some distant spot, far away from Abaddon and the trailer.

They were interrupted by another knock on the trailer door. "Seth! It's time to go!"

"Coming!" Seth called, seeming to return to his place in Abaddon's arms. He swallowed, squaring his shoulders. "I need to go now."

"I'll come with you."

"No." Abaddon felt a ripple in the energy of Seth's soul, like a pebble sinking into a still lake. "You don't have to come."

"I promised I'd be there—"

"At the end."

"Yes. If I'm able, at any rate. And if it's tonight—"

"No." Another ripple. A strange undercurrent that seemed out of place. "No, it won't be tonight."

"You can't know that."

"But I do."

"I should be there—"

"You're exhausted." Seth put his fingers against Abaddon's cheek and leaned forward to kiss him. Abaddon tasted the familiar sweetness, along with a strange hint of salt that was new. Maybe it was only the result of having had sex out of wedlock. "You should rest. I'll be back before you know it."

Then he was out the door, off to the revival. Abaddon debated following, but Seth was right. He was exhausted. He hadn't slept well in ages.

He collapsed onto the bed. The sheets were soaked in Seth's cotton-candy essence, and Abaddon smiled to himself, already halfway to sleep.

He still had his extension. He'd go back to Hell. He'd talk to Baphomet again. He'd come up with a new plan.

One that saved Seth.

Maybe one that saved them both.

———◇◇◇———

He woke in confusion. He was still in Seth's bed. He could have sworn Seth had called his name, but when he looked around, nobody was there.

He glanced outside. It was just after sunset. The tent was lit up like a circus. The revival would still be going, and yet...

There was no music.

His heart tripped into gear.

And then, it came again.

Abaddon, come now!

Not Seth's voice, but Zed's. Abaddon didn't take time to wonder why Zed was calling him or how he'd made his voice echo through the abyss. He burst from the trailer, noticing in the first step or two he wasn't wearing shoes, or a shirt. Easy enough to change that—being a devil had its advantages—and he manifested them as he ran, remembering with sudden clarity the strange ripple in Seth's soul.

That salty taste.

Seth had lied to him. Possibly the first lie he'd ever told, and he'd told it to Abaddon, knowing Abaddon wouldn't be able to keep his promise. Knowing he wouldn't be able to stand idly by when the snakes came.

He burst through the back door of the tent, onto the stage. He'd missed the snakes completely. Seth was in the aisle, his shirt soaked with blood and venom, on his knees in front of a woman in a wheelchair.

"No!" Abaddon ran for him, but Zed caught him at the bottom of the steps.

"Not yet!"

"He didn't think they'd come tonight."

"They wouldn't have," Zed said quietly, "if he hadn't called them."

"He can do that?"

"Apparently, he can. He made me promise I'd get you once they had gone."

"But why? Why would he want to—?"

"I suspect he has his reasons for choosing the time of his death."

Death.

This was Abaddon's fault. Seth was afraid to face his death alone, and so he'd chosen to call the snakes now, before Hell took Abaddon away. If only he hadn't told Seth, and yet what else could he have done?

Grief stabbed at his abdomen, bending him in half. Zed had to hold him up to keep him from falling. "No! Dammit, no! Don't do this!" He'd never felt as helpless as he did now, watching Seth soak up somebody else's disease, knowing it would kill him. It made him furious. He felt the power stir and quake inside him. He could burn the whole revival to the ground. He could kill them all. He could—

Seth turned his head, his blind eyes pinning Abaddon where he stood, blazing with the ferocity of a dying soul. "You promised."

It was only a whisper, but it struck at Abaddon's heart. A sob broke in his chest. He didn't even care that Zed still held him.

It felt like they stayed there forever—Seth on the floor, holding the woman's hands. Zed in the aisle, holding Abaddon up—but it could only have been a minute. Finally, Seth pushed to his feet. Behind him, the woman in the wheelchair rose as well. The crowd cheered. Thaddeus began to proclaim the grace of God. The choir began to sing. Nobody seemed to notice that Seth's sweet, devout life was about to end.

"Go," Zed said softly, letting Abaddon go. "Bring him away from the tent, as quickly as you can. Thaddeus must never know that tonight is different."

Abaddon barely got there in time, catching Seth as he fell. A few of the congregants gasped, backing up.

"Just give them some room!" Thaddeus cried.

The crowd seemed half-afraid, half-jubilant. Voices shouted, "Me! Heal me!"

"Give them space," Thaddeus cried again. "The Lord's touch is a powerful thing—"

Abaddon scooped Seth up in his arms, carrying him up onto the stage, toward the back door of the tent, choking on his tears, hating the sounds of celebration behind him. "You lied to me."

Seth hung limp in his arms, barely able to hold his eyes open. "Had to… Before you were gone…"

Abaddon stumbled out the back door of the tent and toward Seth's trailer. It felt like it was miles away. He'd never make it. Zed was nowhere to be seen.

"Here," Seth whispered. "Stop here."

It was a relief to obey. His whole body was shaking. Abaddon sank to the ground, holding Seth close, crying like a child. "Why did you lie to me? We could have had a few days at least."

Seth shook his head. His face looked almost yellow against the bloody gore of his ruined neck and the shredded collar of his once-white shirt. How many snakes must have come? "It's easier this way."

"Easier for who?"

"I lied about one other thing too."

"What?"

"About who owns my soul."

"No!"

"I give it willingly to you."

"Don't say that!"

"I mean it, Abaddon." He gasped, arching his back as in pain. "I cede my soul—"

"I won't take it!"

"You have to."

A sob tore from Abaddon's chest, and he held Seth tighter. Behind him, the sound of music swelled from the tent, the notes empty and meaningless without Seth's contribution. "I won't!"

"My eyes," Seth whispered, his voice weaker. "Let me see you again. Please."

It took a moment for Abaddon to push his grief aside enough to realize what the words meant. Another moment to gather the strength and the focus, but finally, he placed his fingers against Seth's temple. Tears flowed down his cheeks as readily as the power surged through his fingers, and Seth's pupils at last found focus. He looked directly into Abaddon's eyes, and Abaddon felt the wondrous power of Seth's soul. He felt the scalding flare that told him it was about to burn out forever.

"I love you," Abaddon gasped. "Oh God, I love you so much, I think it's killing me. I didn't even know I could, but I do."

Seth reached up and laid his hand against Abaddon's cheek. "But you don't want to take me with you."

He thought the pain would tear him in half, but he forced himself to maintain contact. To keep Seth's vision intact for just a bit longer. "No. You don't belong where I reside. You deserve better than that."

Seth smiled, looking as peaceful as he ever had. "'And if a kingdom be divided against itself, that kingdom cannot stand. And if a house be divided against itself, that house cannot stand. And if Satan rise up against himself, and be divided, he cannot stand, but hath an end.'"

"You fool," Abaddon sobbed. "Spouting biblical bullshit until the end, you damned fool!"

"'All sins shall be forgiven unto the sons of men.'"

Abaddon lost all control then, over both his emotions and his power. Seth's eyes again lost focus, and Abaddon felt the loss like a knife in his heart. No matter what verses Seth might recite, there was no saving him now. And once he crossed over, he'd be out of Abaddon's reach forever. He needed only to accept the offer of Seth's soul in order for them to be together, but he couldn't do it. He couldn't condemn Seth to an eternity in Hell. Abaddon had to let him go. He couldn't afford to doubt. He couldn't afford to change his mind, no matter how much it hurt. He could do nothing but hold Seth and weep.

"Peace and love to you, brother," Seth whispered. "Peace and love."

And Abaddon continued to hold him as the glorious wonder of Seth's soul faded into darkness.

◆◇◆

He didn't know how long he sat there, clutching Seth's limp body.

He'd feel this pain for an eternity. It was a worse punishment than living in Hell.

"Abaddon." Zed was suddenly there, kneeling in front of him, gripping Abaddon's arms, shaking him, although his voice was hushed. "Come with me. There isn't much time."

Abaddon made himself look up. He could barely force his numb mind to work. "Wh-what?"

Zed gripped him harder. His eyes seemed to blaze as he leaned closer. "I know what you are, Abaddon, Harvester of Souls. And I know what you were before. Now, it is time for you to know me." It wasn't just his eyes that were blazing. All around him, Abaddon detected a faint glow, burning brighter as he tried to focus on it. And peeking up over Zed's shoulders, he caught the faint outline of white wings.

No wonder Zed's dark eyes had always seemed to find him, even when he drifted in the abyss. No wonder he'd been able to call to Abaddon when Seth couldn't.

"You're an angel?"

"Yes, and I can still save him, but not here, where somebody might see. Thaddeus can never know that this night is different from all the other times the snakes appeared." In the blink of an eye, the glow was gone, leaving only plain old Zed. He stood, whirling toward Seth's trailer. "Quickly!"

Too stunned to do more, Abaddon obeyed, lifting Seth and following Zed across the dark expanse of grass to Seth's trailer and through the door.

"Lay him on the bed."

Abaddon didn't want to let go of him, but Zed took Seth's body from his arms.

"It's too late." Abaddon's voice was hoarse from crying. "Even for you—"

"Not yet, it isn't." Zed laid Seth on the bed and crouched over him, his hands on Seth's head.

"If you know what I am, then you know what I can do. I felt—" He choked on the words, fighting back a sob. "I felt his soul leave."

"The boy's heart has stopped, but his soul is as strong as ever." Zed's head was lowered, as if in prayer, his eyes closed. "What you felt was your own powers waning."

"But—"

"He told you himself before he died. 'If Satan rise up against himself, and be divided, he cannot stand, but hath an end.' He gambled with the devil, and he won. Now be silent and let me work!"

Abaddon's knees gave out. He sank to the floor, thinking back over that moment when he'd held Seth's dying body. He'd been using his power to let Seth see one more time before he died, and it had failed, leaving Seth as blind as before. Abaddon had assumed it was grief clouding his abilities. He'd felt Seth's glorious soul fade away, but now...

He reached for the abyss, for the tunnel of darkness leading back to his cubicle in the Soul Acquisition Department. He reached for the familiar void that had become his home.

There was nothing there.

He turned next to the well of power that resided where his soul had once been—the power that let him grant wishes in exchange for souls—but found he no longer knew the way. He felt lost inside his own body. His heart still beat. The weight of grief hung heavy in his chest. His tear-burned eyes felt like they'd been blasted with sand. But he no longer knew the path that led to that devilish place inside of him.

He lifted his hands, staring at his shaking fingers.

No power lingered there.

He looked up at Zed, stunned. Zed was leaning over Seth's still form, his hands on Seth's head, mumbling in a language Abaddon no longer recognized. The glow had returned, along with Zed's wings. It enveloped Zed and Seth both, pulsing faintly.

Abaddon pushed himself from his spot on the floor and sat next to Seth on the bed. Seth's hand wasn't cold, as he'd expected. It was as warm as ever. He wrapped his fingers around Seth's slender wrist, feeling for a pulse.

Hardly daring to hope.

He watched in awe as the scars and open wounds on Seth's neck began to fade. The pink slowly returned to his cheeks. The faint beat of blood in Seth's veins tickled Abaddon's fingertips, and his chest began to rise and fall in slow, easy breaths.

"You did it!"

The glow around Zed faded and he finally lifted his eyes.

"Zed," Abaddon said, having finally figured it out. "Zedekiel. Angel of mercy and freedom."

"It is I."

"You could have healed him all along."

"No. I can only heal mortals, and I couldn't make him mortal until the inhuman part of him died."

Abaddon thought Zed was dodging the issue, but he wasn't sure he cared. He leaned over Seth, touching his cheek. He still sensed Seth's soul, that sweet purity that had drawn him to Seth to begin with, but not with the clarity and desperation he'd had before. The soul hunger was gone. In its place was only love and tenderness.

"He's mortal now," Zed said quietly. "You both are. Do you understand what that means?"

"He won't be able to heal anybody anymore."

"Right."

"And we both have our souls."

"Yes, and a clean slate. But that also means you can both die."

"Will the snakes still come?"

"Not like before, but he may encounter more of them than the average mortal. And he's no longer immune. It is your job to keep him safe."

"I'll protect him or die trying."

"That's as much as I can ask."

Abaddon held Seth's hand. He brushed his fingers down Seth's cheek. Seth didn't even stir. He glanced up at Zed. "Are you his father?"

Zed's laughter was loud and deep. His teeth flashed brightly against his dark skin. "A boy as soft and pink as he? You think he came from my loins?"

Abaddon was both embarrassed and annoyed. "I don't know how angel genetics work!"

Zed laughed again. "No, his father was one of you. Or at least, one like you used to be. His mother..." He sighed. "His mother was like me. She was my friend."

"What happened?"

"What always happens. They fell in love." He shook his head. "Even angels seem to go for the bad boys."

"Where are they now?"

"His mother was cast out as punishment. She resides as a mortal now, with no memory of Seth or his sire."

"And what about the father? Where is he?"

"I cannot say. I know only that he hasn't been seen in the mortal realm since that time. He broke many rules to stay with her through the pregnancy. Whether he was discovered and his Earth-traveling powers revoked, or whether he simply doesn't care is anybody's guess, but I suspect the former."

"Has it happened before? Angels and devils reproducing, I mean."

"Only a couple dozen times, in all these eons. The results are always unpredictable. Some become prophets and saints. Some go the other way and do unspeakable things. But all of them die before their twenty-fifth birthdays."

"Is that why you decided to watch over him?"

"I was the only one left who knew of his existence. I watched from a distance, at first. He was safe enough with the Rainbow people, even after his father died. But then, when he was about to turn nineteen, he became restless. He began talking of leaving the congregation and going out into the world on his own."

"He told me about that."

Zed shook his head. "I couldn't let that happen. The risk was too great. So I came here, where I could watch him better."

"That's why he went blind. He told me it happened on his nineteenth birthday, the day you arrived."

"Yes. Partly I did it to discourage him from leaving. But given his extraordinary heritage, I feared he'd be able to see my true form." He chuckled. "Of course, if I'd left him his sight, he would have seen what you were immediately as well."

Abaddon couldn't help but wonder how different things might have been if Seth had recognized the danger he was in from the beginning. "If you knew what I was, why on earth did you let me get so close to him?"

"I admit, I was horrified that first time you appeared. Seth told me how he'd gambled his soul against another. He laughed about it, having no understanding that the contest had been real. I told him he must never partake in such folly again."

"He didn't listen."

Zed shook his head. "I know. He said he wasn't a child, and that I worried too much."

"And later?"

"I was torn. I wanted to keep him as far away from you as possible. But the truth is, you made him happy. You gave him what he's always longed for—the simple joy of falling in love—and he was brighter than I'd ever seen him." Zed shrugged, looking out the trailer's small window toward the revival tent. "It felt wrong to forbid him that happiness, especially knowing his days were limited. I still feared his feelings for you would be his downfall, but later... I began to have faith that you would do the right thing."

Abaddon rubbed his hand through his hair. It was strange, realizing that this form he'd adopted was now permanent. "How could you have faith in a devil?"

The corner of Zed's mouth twitched up in a grin. "Your past may be lost to you, Brother Abaddon, but not to me. You were once a good man."

Abaddon's heart clenched. "I was? But how—"

"You fell in love with the wrong person. That person betrayed you, and when a devil asked for your soul, you asked for one simple thing in return."

Abaddon swallowed hard, wondering. "What was it? Revenge?"

"No. You asked for a ticket home."

It was strange how something so simple—something lost to him forever—could hurt so much. "Home? Where was home?"

"In Buxton."

"I'm English?" Funny, how it had never occurred to him to wonder at his nationality.

"You were, yes. And quite proud of it, at the time. Between that and your broken heart, you decided to join the army. And so on May 1st, 1915, you boarded the RMS Lusitania, bound for Liverpool."

Understanding dawned. "And she was sunk by a German sub."

"Exactly."

Abaddon shook his head. "That explains why I hate the ocean."

"It does." Zed chuckled, shaking his head. "You were a pretty lousy devil, you know."

"So I've heard."

"I think maybe it's because your conscience never quite died. Would you like to know your true name?"

"Oh, man." Abaddon rubbed his hand roughly over his face and considered the question. He wasn't sure if he understood his reluctance, but he decided to trust his heart. "Thanks, but no. I think I'll stick with Abaddon."

"A wise choice. You have paid the price for your foolishness, and now you will never forget that it's because of Seth that you have a second chance." He stood, looking somehow more regal in his purple boubou now that Abaddon knew he was an angel. "The revival will end soon. After a healing as spectacular as that, we'll have to leave as soon as possible, preferably before dawn. There's a lot of work to be done. Wake him up, but be gentle about it."

"I will." Zed was at the trailer door before Abaddon stopped him. "Hey, Zed? How in the world are you going to explain all this to your boss?"

Zed's laughter was deep. He still sounded like James Earl Jones. "My cubicle is many floors from His office. It has been eons since I've seen Him." He shook his head, rubbing his chin in thought. "I don't know what Hell is like, Abaddon, but in Heaven, there's an awful lot of paperwork to be done. And if one or two reports get lost in the shuffle?" He held up his hands, smiling. "How can one single, overworked angel be to blame?"

Chapter Eleven
A Serious Shortage of Potato Chips and Beds

Zed left, and Abaddon sat for a while, just watching Seth sleep. Seth had gambled his soul, not for his own gain, but for Abaddon's. And somehow, they'd both won.

He leaned closer, kissing Seth's forehead. His eyebrows. His cheek. And when Seth finally began to stir, Abaddon moved to his lips.

"Abaddon?"

"Shh. Everything's okay. Just rest for now."

"I thought I died."

"You did."

"I thought— Oh!" It was a gasp, a startled sound of wonder, his grip surprisingly strong on Abaddon's wrist, and Abaddon drew back in alarm.

"What is it?"

Seth's eyes were wide, and for once, they found Abaddon's gaze immediately. "I can see!"

Abaddon smiled, thinking how he should have anticipated that. "'I will make darkness light before them, and crooked things straight.'"

"And you?" Seth asked, placing his hand against Abaddon's cheek. "Your eyes are normal. And they're beautiful. Are you a crooked thing made straight?"

Abaddon took his hand and held it to his chest. "I am a damned man who's been saved."

It felt like there was so much more to say, but Zed's deep voice reached them from somewhere across the grounds. "I don't care that it's late! We must leave tonight!"

"Oh no," Seth groaned. "He wants us gone by dawn again, doesn't he?"

"You guessed it."

"I should help."

"No, you should rest."

"Please don't start treating me the way they do, Abaddon, like I'm some kind of liability. I have to do my part."

Abaddon sighed. "Fair enough. But you should at least change your shirt before you go." He fingered the blood-soaked collar. "I think this one's just about had it."

Seth needed a bit of help getting up, but he was steady enough once he was on his feet. "I can't believe how happy I am to see the inside of this crappy little trailer." He blushed a bit as he stripped out of his shirt, as if embarrassed at having Abaddon see him. He took a clean one out of a drawer and ducked into the bathroom to clean up. For a minute, Abaddon heard the water running, but even after it turned off, Seth didn't emerge. He seemed to be taking forever. The bathroom door was open, so Abaddon peeked inside.

Seth was simply standing shirtless at the mirror, staring at himself.

"Is everything the way you remembered?" Abaddon asked.

Seth closed his eyes. He touched his neck, feeling the smooth, unscarred skin there with shaking fingers. When he spoke, his voice was barely a whisper. "Something's different, isn't it? I'm different. I don't understand what's happened."

Abaddon considered Seth's parentage. His transition from something supernatural to a mere mortal. "There's a lot you should know." But the din of the revivalists trying to pack up camp was getting louder, the commotion moving their way. "I'll explain once we're on the way, okay?"

Seth nodded, taking a deep breath. "Okay." He pulled the clean T-shirt over his head. Abaddon handed him one of his many scarves.

"It might be easier than explaining how you're suddenly healed."

Seth nodded and wrapped it around his neck without checking the mirror. Some habits would take a while to break. He looked more at ease once he was dressed.

"All I'm thinking about is myself." He stepped closer and put his fingers on Abaddon's cheek. "How are you?"

Abaddon put his hand over Seth's and turned his face to kiss Seth's fingers. "I have no money. No job. No ID. No clothes except the ones I'm wearing. But I am happier than I have ever been."

"What will you do?" Seth asked. "Will you stay?"

"I will do anything you ask of me."

Seth's smile was slow and sweet. "Maybe we can talk about that on the way too."

"Good idea."

They made it to the trailer door before Seth turned to face him again.

"This may sound stupid, but...does my soul still belong to God?"

Abaddon laughed. "Without a doubt." He pulled Seth into his arms and kissed him. "And mine belongs to you."

It took nearly four hours to pack up camp. Abaddon had a feeling it would have been a bit less if Seth had stayed hidden in his trailer, but everybody could tell he'd miraculously regained his sight, and that slowed things considerably.

Finally, at one o'clock in the morning they were ready to go.

"I've driven for you since you were nineteen," Zed said as he handed Seth the keys to his truck. "But you no longer need my services."

Seth laughed and handed them to Abaddon. "It might be best if you drive, for now. It's been a while since I was behind the wheel."

Besides, he was obviously exhausted. Zed caught a ride in one of the semi trucks, leaving Abaddon alone with Seth in the cab of his pickup. And there, he explained it all—Seth's parentage, Zed's true nature, and the fact that Seth was now one hundred percent human.

"So my blindness wasn't punishment after all?" Seth said, when Abaddon was done. "Not from God, at least. It was just so I wouldn't leave."

"And so you wouldn't see Zed's true form."

"I guess that means he'll go back to Heaven soon."

Abaddon glanced over at him, but couldn't read his expression. He had a feeling his spectacular night vision might be the one part of being a devil he missed. "Probably, yes."

"And you? Will you leave too?"

"Only if you ask me to."

"And if I asked you to leave, but to take me with you?"

"To see the Grand Canyon?"

"Yes."

"What about your brother and the revival?"

Seth shrugged. "He'll be disappointed, but I think he'll understand. The ministry has always been more his calling than mine."

"Maybe Zed can send him a vision or something. Mortals always go for those."

Seth leaned his head against the passenger window. It was a minute before he spoke again. "Will we be okay, Abaddon?"

"What do you mean?"

"I don't have a lot, you know. Just this truck, and that trailer we're towing. I have a violin, a guitar, a couple of keyboards, and about four thousand dollars."

"I have nothing at all but my devotion to you."

"It isn't much to start a life with, is it?"

"It'll be enough."

Seth laughed, shaking his head. "I'm suddenly wishing I'd taken you up on that golden fiddle."

By the time they stopped at six a.m., Seth had been asleep in the passenger seat for three hours, and Abaddon could barely keep his eyes open. Abaddon had a quick conversation with Zed before stumbling into Seth's trailer. He wanted nothing more than to fall into bed with Seth in his arms.

Seth blushed furiously when Abaddon began stripping to his skivvies. He took his own pajamas into the bathroom to change. He couldn't seem to meet Abaddon's eyes when he emerged. He climbed hesitantly into bed, but when Abaddon reached for him, he resisted.

"What's wrong?"

"Don't take this wrong, but, uh…no sifting, okay?"

"Sifting?" Abaddon was so tired it took him a moment to make the connection. He chuckled, pulling Seth close, happy just to feel the warmth of his body. "Don't worry. I'm too tired to sift anyway."

He slept soundly until just after noon. When he woke, Seth was nowhere to be seen. That troubled him. He had a feeling Seth was avoiding him, although he tried to convince himself he was being foolish. He took advantage of the trailer's tiny shower. When he emerged, he found a familiar devil in the kitchen, rifling through the trailer's refrigerator.

"Damien's dick, I've never seen so much yogurt! Don't they have any potato chips?"

"Baphomet? What are you doing here?"

"Abaddon!" Baphomet slammed the fridge shut and turned to greet him. "Do you have any idea how hard it was to find you, you lousy son of a bitch?"

But he was smiling as he said it and Abaddon found himself laughing, pulling Baphomet into a hug and pounding him on the back.

"All right, all right. It's good to see you too. No need to go to pieces on me."

Abaddon laughed again and let him go. "I hope you're not here for my soul. I have no intention of making that mistake again."

"After you found a way out?" Baphomet shook his head. "I'd never do that to a friend. Even a shitty friend who left me stranded alone in Hell."

"I appreciate that." But then an even worse thought occurred to him. "And not Seth, either. Tell me you're not here for Seth."

"I'm not here for Seth either, I promise. Sugary souls have never been to my taste. I do have a question, though."

"You want to know how I did it."

"Well, yeah. Me and every other devil."

Abaddon told him, and in the end, Baphomet sighed. "So all I have to do is get some fool to fall in love with me and to willingly cede his soul with nothing asked in return, and then I have to decline it?"

"Doesn't sound so hard, right?"

Baphomet scratched the back of his neck. "I imagine trickery won't work, either. Knowing the rules of Heaven and Hell, it probably has to be true love." He met Abaddon's eyes reluctantly. "You must have found the real thing, my friend."

Abaddon smiled, thinking of Seth. "I think I did."

Baphomet groaned. "You always were a disgusting sap. I think I'll get out of here before you start waxing poetic."

"I'll miss seeing you," Abaddon told him. "It sounds ridiculous, but it's true."

"Oh, you'll see me from time to time." Baphomet clapped Abaddon on the shoulder. "I have every intention of hassling you whenever my schedule permits."

He found Seth outside, his neck wrapped in a scarf as usual, hanging a load of wet laundry on the line. One line held sheets. The next line held clothes. A few of the items were obviously Seth's, but several of them looked far too big.

"They're for you," Seth said, when he saw Abaddon studying them. "Donated by the Rainbow Revivalists. I figured you'd get tired of wearing the same clothes every day."

"You figured right." Abaddon pinched a pair of wet corduroys. He hoped they were more comfortable than they looked. "How exactly did you explain my lack of clothing?"

"I didn't."

"You let them guess and then agreed when they said something reasonable?"

Seth grinned at him as he hung the last shirt. "The prevailing theory is that the car you were living out of was stolen, along with everything you own."

"Makes sense to me." He took Seth's hand and pulled him close. Seth came, but kept his eyes on Abaddon's Adam's apple, as if he wasn't used to looking into his eyes yet. Abaddon touched the scarf. "Still hiding your neck?"

Seth shrugged uncomfortably. "Like you said, it's easier than explaining why I don't have scars anymore. It'll only be until we go."

"Have you talked to your brother about that?"

Seth smiled, looking sinfully mischievous. "Yes. It seems he had some kind of vision last night. Some mysterious angel with a deep, booming voice told him my healing had run its course. He said it's time for us to part ways, for a while at least. He's been inspired to give up the revival and take up a growing ministry in Georgia."

Abaddon laughed. He'd have to thank Zed later. "I told you mortals always go for those angelic visions."

"I almost feel guilty." He didn't look too penitent though. He looked happier than Abaddon had ever seen him. "So are you ready to leave?"

"Whenever you are."

"I was thinking tomorrow morning."

"Sounds good to me."

Now that he was rested, being this close to Seth was driving him crazy. His soul hunger was gone, but he wanted Seth as much as ever. He leaned close, brushing his lips over Seth's, but Seth pushed him gently away.

Abaddon frowned. Was it only the public display of affection that bothered Seth, or was there something else?

"You know I love you, right?"

Seth nodded, still not meeting Abaddon's eyes.

"Then what's wrong? Is this not what you want anymore? I know we haven't known each other that long. Maybe I'm pushing for something you don't really want. Maybe it's too much, too soon."

Seth shook his head. "No. That's not it at all. It's just..." He chewed his lip for a minute, glancing around. Then he took Abaddon's hand and pulled him behind the damp sheet, granting them a semblance of privacy. "You've lived a long time. You've probably seen a lot. And now, you're free to do anything you want."

"Yes, and the only thing I want is to be with you."

"Are you sure?"

"Absolutely positive."

Seth smiled, still looking unsure of himself, but a bit more confident than before. "The thing is, my trailer is really small."

"I've noticed."

"And there's only one bed."

"I've noticed that too."

Seth's cheeks were beginning to turn pink, but he finally met Abaddon's eyes. "I've spent twenty-two years living by God's commands. I don't intend to stop now. After everything that's happened, my faith is stronger than ever."

"I can understand that."

"And that one night..." Seth let Abaddon pull him close again. He brushed his fingers over the collar of Abaddon's shirt. "I was dying, Abaddon."

"I know."

"But now, I'm not."

"I know that too."

Seth blinked at him, waiting. "Don't you see what I'm saying?"

"No." Abaddon shook his head, confused. "Is it me? You were willing to settle for me when I was the only option, but now you have your whole life ahead of you. Maybe you want to find somebody better? Somebody closer to your age who shares your beliefs—"

"No! No, you're not understanding me at all." Seth bit his lip, and Abaddon feared he was fighting tears. "I don't need you to share my beliefs, but I need you to respect them."

"I do."

"But Abaddon—"

"Is this because I laugh at you when you throw bible quotes at me?"

"No!" Seth smacked him lightly on the chest, half laughing, half crying. "I don't care about that. But how can we— I can't—" He gestured helplessly toward the trailer, looking so hopelessly frustrated that Abaddon was tempted to laugh again. "There's only one bed!"

And suddenly, like somebody had flipped a light switch, Abaddon saw the problem. And the solution. It was so simple, and yet so obvious, it made him laugh out loud.

"What?" Seth asked, trying to pull away. "You're laughing at me again."

"No," Abaddon assured him, holding him tight, refusing to let him get away. He made Seth meet his eyes. "You're right, there's only one bed, and I don't want it to be your bed. I want it to be our bed. I'd drag you in there right now, if I thought you'd let me. But despite what you think, I do respect you. I may not share your beliefs, but I love you for having them." He wasn't sure he was explaining it well though. Seth still looked confused. "I can tell you that in all my years in Hell, I never met a single soul who was there just for having sex. But I don't want anything between us to make you doubt yourself, and there's only one way to make sure what happens in that one bed doesn't feel like a sin to you."

For a moment, Seth held very still, soaking that in. The embarrassment on his face began to look like hope. "Do you mean it?"

"Of course I mean it!"

"I don't want you to feel like I'm forcing you into anything."

"Are you kidding? I love you so much I can hardly stand it. 'But if they have no self-control, let them marry; for it is better to marry than to burn with passion.'" He laughed, debating that. "Although frankly, I don't see why we can't do both."

Seth's smile had never been brighter. "Get married *and* burn with passion?"

"Exactly. What do you say?"

"I think I like that idea."

And this time when Abaddon kissed him, he didn't pull away.

They sealed the deal that very day, with Thaddeus presiding. And that night, Seth left Abaddon absolutely no doubts about his feelings. They made love with a quiet passion that left them both shaken, kissing away each other's tears, trembling in each other's arms.

Abaddon had no idea what Heaven was like, but he couldn't imagine it was better than what he'd found.

The next morning, they climbed into the truck, Seth driving, and Abaddon in the passenger seat, wearing some of the revivalists' donated clothing.

It turned out corduroys really were more comfortable than they looked.

"I made us a list," Seth said, handing Abaddon a lined piece of paper that had been ripped from a spiral-bound notebook. "It's flexible though. There's no particular order or anything. We can mix it up. Maybe do some of them more than once."

Abaddon read it, and all he could do was laugh. He unwound Seth's scarf and tossed it aside before pulling Seth into a kiss.

He still tasted like cotton candy and honey.

"I think it's perfect."

And as they started down the road, he taped the paper to the dashboard.

> *Grand Canyon*
> *Star Wars*
> *Bryce and Zion National Parks*
> *Disneyland*
> *Lots and lots of sifting*

About the Author

Marie Sexton's first novel, *Promises*, was published in January 2010. Since then, she's published roughly thirty novels, novellas, and short stories, all featuring men who fall in love with other men. Her works include contemporary romance, science fiction, fantasy, historicals, and a few odd genre mash-ups. Marie is the recipient of multiple Rainbow Awards, as well as the CRW Award of Excellence in 2012. Her books have been translated into seven languages.

Marie lives in Colorado. She's a fan of just about anything that involves muscular young men piling on top of each other. In particular, she loves the Denver Broncos and enjoys going to the games with her husband. Her imaginary friends often tag along. Marie has one daughter, one cat, and one dog, all of whom seem bent on destroying what remains of her sanity. She loves them anyway.

Marie also writes dark dystopian fantasy under the name A.M. Sexton.

Website: mariesexton.net
Facebook: www.facebook.com/MarieSexton.author
Twitter: twitter.com/MarieSexton

Read on for an excerpt of Marie Sexton's

Winter Oranges

Chapter One

It was easy to believe the house was haunted. After acting for most of his life, Jason Walker's first thought upon seeing the home he'd purchased virtually sight unseen was that it would have been a perfect place to film an Amityville remake.

A little far from Amity, but hey, Hollywood had never been a stickler for rules.

Or honesty.

Jason put his car in park and killed the engine. Gravel crunched as his friend Dylan's rental car rolled to a stop next to him. They climbed out of their vehicles and stood side by side, leaning against Jason's front bumper, staring up at his new abode.

Dylan whistled, long and low, then shook his head. "This place is creepy as hell."

"It's just the light." Even a washed-up actor like Jason knew lighting could make or break a scene. The pictures he'd seen online of the house had been taken in full sunlight in October, with the majestic glory of autumn on all sides, the gold- and scarlet-leaved trees nearer the house backed by the evergreens of the surrounding forest. But now, only a week into November, the eerie orange glow of twilight fell on bare branches, and the pines seemed droopy and forlorn. None of it was doing this house any favors.

Still, Dylan had a point. The house was creepy. Something about the lone, low window over the second floor's covered patio. Something about the house's quiet isolation, and the thin white curtains hanging uniformly in every window. Or maybe it was the detached garage with its guesthouse on top, sitting like a forgotten toy off to the left.

"How old is it?" Dylan asked.

"It was built in the '90s."

"The 1890s?" Dylan was incredulous. The idea of spending money on anything so old was obviously beyond his comprehension.

"No. The 1990s."

"It looks older."

"It's supposed to." His real estate agent, Sydney Bell, had called the house an American foursquare revival. Jason didn't know what that meant and didn't care. The price was right, the house was fully furnished, and its relative seclusion in the mountainous region of Idaho's panhandle would make it harder for tabloid photographers to find him.

"They intentionally made it look old?" Dylan asked, as if it was the most absurd thing he'd heard all day.

"They copied an older style of architecture."

"Huh." Dylan scratched his chin and threw Jason a smart-assed grin. "Retro. Like you."

Jason laughed, because that's what Dylan expected. "Fuck you." He pushed off the bumper of his car, rattling his keys in his hand. "Let's see what it's like inside."

The second story extended out over the first like an overbite, creating a covered front porch that ran the length of the house. "A veranda," Sydney had called it. The front door opened into a hallway, although Jason suspected Sydney would have said it was a foyer. Or maybe a vestibule. To the right lay a large living room, furnished in what could only be called cozy-grandma style, with lots of flowers and overstuffed cushions. A stack of moving boxes stood in the center of the floor, having been left there the previous day by the moving company, working under Sydney's direction. To the left of the foyer sat the dining room, through which they could see the kitchen. Jason knew a mudroom and pantry made up the back half of the area. Directly ahead of where they stood by the front door, a bathroom and the staircase leading up completed the ground floor.

No ghosts, though. Not so far, at least.

"Who the hell picked out that couch?" Dylan asked.

"The previous owner, I guess." In truth, Jason hadn't cared much what the furniture looked like. Sydney had promised him it was all in decent condition. Jason was just happy he didn't have to go wandering around town searching for a damn table to eat at, or a chair to sit in while he watched TV. He'd had Sydney stock the kitchen with a few essentials too, assuring he wouldn't have to go grocery shopping for a few days at least. The last thing he needed was for somebody in Coeur d'Alene to discover the child star turned B-list actor known to the public as Jadon Walker Buttermore had moved in to their small community. The longer he remained anonymous, the better.

Dylan scowled at the couch as if it had personally offended him. Knowing Dylan and his neo-minimalist style, it probably had. "It's like something my grandma would have bought."

Jason laughed. "What? You have something against giant pink roses?"

"On a couch? Yeah, I do. And so should you."

Jason sat down on the sofa and leaned back. He searched with his left hand and found the lever to extend the footrest. He reclined the backrest and smiled up at Dylan. "It's not bad, actually."

"You should have let me furnish it for you."

"Yeah, right." Jason sat upright again, shoving the footrest closed with his heels. "I'd have ended up with one designer chair that cost more than my car. And it wouldn't even have been comfortable."

Dylan's laugh was sudden and loud in the confines of the quiet house. "Boy, you don't think much of me, do you?"

That wasn't true. That wasn't true at all, and he suspected Dylan knew it, but Dylan always did this to him, asking questions that seemed to dare Jason to blurt out how he really felt. Jason chose to ignore most of them, this one included. "Come on. Let's check out the rest."

Although the house was more than twenty years old, the kitchen had been updated and included all new chrome appliances and a trash compactor that Sydney swore was top-of-the-line and quiet as a whisper. Jason didn't bother to test the claim.

The second floor held a tiny bathroom and four bedrooms, one in each corner, which Jason supposed was what gave the foursquare its name. A stairway led to a long, slope-ceilinged attic bedroom. At the far end, the single narrow window Jason had noticed upon arrival allowed a bit of light to creep inside. It was a sad, empty room, and they didn't linger.

"Whoever lived here sure did love flowers," Dylan said as they scoped out the first couple of bedrooms on the second floor. "Wallpaper, bedspreads, pictures. Even the rug in the bathroom has roses on it. And they're all pink."

"It could be worse."

"How?"

"Uh . . ." Jason stopped, considering. "I'm not sure, to be honest."

They ended their tour, by some unspoken agreement, in the master bedroom. It was the one room Jason'd had refurnished before his arrival. He'd chosen the furniture himself—online, of course—and Sydney had made sure everything would be ready when he arrived. His new room held a large oak dresser, a chest of drawers, and a love seat, which he knew would end up a depository for not-quite-dirty laundry. A king-sized bed covered with a thick down comforter sat against the wall, between two nightstands.

Dylan pointed to the glass-paned door in the corner of the room. "This goes to that patio we could see from the front yard?"

"It does."

The two front bedrooms shared a covered porch that sat dead center of the front of the house, directly below the attic window. It was a strange setup, a throwback to when husbands and wives had separate quarters. The porch would have allowed them to cross to each other's room without alerting the children, except this house had been built at the end of the twentieth century, making the floor plan an anachronism.

Dylan opened the door, and Jason followed him outside. They still wore their jackets, but now the sun had set and the November evening felt cooler than before.

"There's a room over the garage too?" Dylan asked.

"Yep, bed and bath." They stood surveying the building in question from their vantage point on the porch. It was eerily silent.

"Well, is it everything you dreamed?"

Yes. Standing there with Dylan, out of sight of everybody else in the world was exactly what he dreamed about, nearly every night.

Not that he'd ever admit it out loud.

Instead, Jason nodded, then asked, as casually as he could, "You're staying the night, right?"

Dylan grinned and stepped closer to slide his arm around Jason's waist. "I didn't come all this way to see your house."

Jason's relief felt almost tangible, so sudden and strong he wondered if Dylan sensed it. He hoped not. He hoped the darkness hid his pathetic happiness at knowing Dylan was staying. They'd been friends for more than ten years. They'd shared a bed more times than Jason could count. Dylan may have suspected Jason's true feelings, but Jason did his best to never confirm them, especially since Dylan avoided genuine emotions and commitment the way Jason avoided anybody with a press badge hanging around their neck.

Still, Jason rejoiced as Dylan pulled him close. He sank gratefully into the warmth of Dylan's kiss, comfortable in his friend's arms. He grew breathless as Dylan began fighting with the buttons of Jason's jeans.

"Let's do it here," Dylan whispered.

Jason glanced around in alarm, searching for the telltale wink of light reflecting off a camera lens. "Somebody will see."

"There's nobody around. That's why we're in the wilds of Idaho, remember?"

Jason's protests dwindled as Dylan sank to his knees, pulling Jason's pants halfway down his hips as he did. He traced his tongue up Jason's erection. "God, Jase. It's been too long."

"I know." Way too long since he'd had Dylan to himself. Too many lonely nights since he'd felt Dylan's touch. He'd been in love with his friend for longer than he cared to admit, but this was the first time in months they'd been alone together. Still, he was hesitant to do anything out in the open. "Dylan, wait. I—" His words died as Dylan wrapped his lips around Jason's glans. "Oh God."

Dylan sucked him in deep, stalling for moment with his nose pressed against Jason's pubic bone. Then, finally, he began to move, sliding his warm mouth up and down Jason's length. Jason gripped the cold porch railing with one hand, tangled the fingers of the other into Dylan's heavily moussed hair, and tried to lose himself to the pleasure of being sucked by the man he loved. He breathed deep, willing the tension away. Doing his best to banish the pressure of trying to make it in Hollywood and failing, of never living up to what was expected. He tried to forget it all. To simply revel in the pure joy of being with Dylan here and now, knowing they had one full night together, just the two of them. No other struggling actors or desperate starlets. No two-bit directors or double-crossing producers. And above all, no media waiting to catch them with their pants down.

Literally.

But as good as it was being with Dylan, the real world always intruded. His house was set back half an acre from the road, but anybody who came up the drive would be able to see them. The No Trespassing signs wouldn't mean a thing to a photographer hoping for a scoop.

Jason moaned—part pleasure, part disappointment that even now he couldn't relax—and opened his eyes. He kept his hand on Dylan's head as he surveyed the tree line, his chest tight with anxiety at what he might find.

But the grounds around the house—*his* house, he had to remind himself—were dark and still and silent. Nobody lingered there.

Yes, this could really happen. Jason almost laughed at the realization. He imagined being fucked by Dylan right there on the porch. The thought thrilled him, and his throaty moan made Dylan speed up, his ministrations gaining a new urgency as he sucked Jason's cock. In the low light on the porch, Jason could barely make out the movement of Dylan's hand between his legs as he stroked himself.

Did they have any lube handy? Or condoms?

Fuck it. Just this for now. I'll let him suck me here, where only the moon can see. We'll have time for the rest later.

He surveyed the yard again, his eyes half-closed, his breath quick and labored as his orgasm neared. He peered past their parked cars. Found the garage. Followed its lines up toward the second-story guesthouse and its single window—

"Holy shit!" Jason jumped back, away from the porch railing, away from Dylan, trying to clumsily pull his pants up and hide himself against the wall.

"What the hell, Jase?" Dylan's voice was low and hoarse.

"There was somebody—" But there wasn't. Jason swore he'd seen a face in the window of the apartment over the garage, but now it stood empty except for the unmoving curtains. Jason swallowed hard, willing his heart to stop pounding. He pointed with a shaking hand toward the garage. "I thought I saw somebody in the guesthouse."

"I've never met anybody as paranoid as you." Dylan pushed himself up from his knees, his pants still hanging open, his erect cock sticking into the night air like some kind of ridiculous talisman. "Not that it isn't justified, but . . ." He gestured to the empty lawn. "There's nobody there."

"I thought I saw—"

"What? A photographer?"

Jason shook his head, holding his pants closed around his waning erection, trying to sort through his thoughts. Had he imagined it? "It was a man."

"Did he have a camera?"

The question took him aback. "No," he said, almost surprised at his own answer. He'd seen only a face. Not even a full face, to be honest. Only the pale suggestion of eyes and a chin, and lips held in a comical O of surprise.

But now, the window was empty. The curtains weren't even swaying. The room over the garage was pitch dark.

"Do you want me to go check?" Dylan asked with the accommodating condescension of a father offering to check for monsters under his teenage daughter's bed.

"No." Jason took a deep breath and squared his shoulders, feigning a bravado he didn't feel. "You're right. There's nobody there. I must have been seeing things."

Dylan grinned and moved closer, wrapping his arms around him. "You need to relax, JayWalk."

It was the press's nickname for Jason. He hated it, although it didn't sound quite so ridiculous when Dylan said it. "I'm trying."

"You want a drink?"

"That won't help."

"Some weed?" He kissed Jason's neck, pushing his erection insistently against him. "Poppers? A Valium? I have some in my bag. Tell me what you need, baby, and I'll get it. You know that. Anything for you."

Anything.

As long as it was only for tonight.

Anything he needed, but only until morning.

"Let's go inside," Jason said. "I have a brand-new bed in there, you know."

Dylan's laugh was throaty and gratifying. "Then let's go break it in."

Jason followed him inside, glancing once toward the guesthouse over the garage.

Nobody there.

Jason woke to birds chirping happily outside the window. Sunlight was streaming through the thin white curtains, making the entire room feel like a midmorning dream. Dylan slept next to him, his bare back rising and falling with his soft snores. For a while, Jason simply watched him, remembering the night before. Reliving how good it felt to fall asleep next to the man he loved.

If only it could be like this every day.

But no. Dylan would go back to California, and Jason would be left alone in a house that was way too big for him.

He was looking forward to it. Not to Dylan leaving, of course. That'd break his heart, like it always did. But after that, there'd be only him, the house, and the bliss of seclusion. People often said privacy was the last luxury. Jason knew it was true. After a lifetime in the limelight—or chasing the limelight, at any rate—he'd learned that privacy was a commodity more precious than gold, as unattainable as stardom and fame, rarer than real breasts in porn. Privacy was the great white whale, and Jason was determined to harpoon that beast and make it his.

Buying the house had been the first step.

He climbed out of bed and considered what to wear. Of course, the closet and all the drawers were empty. They'd never gotten around to bringing his suitcases in from the car. Some of the boxes in the living room held clothes, but he'd didn't relish the idea of digging through them naked. He put on the jeans he'd worn the day before and went barefoot down the stairs in search of coffee. He waited until it was brewing to check his cell phone. No messages from Natalie Reuben, his agent. That meant no pictures had surfaced of him and Dylan on the porch.

Not yet, at least.

He took his coffee out onto the veranda. Movement flashed in his peripheral vision, but when he turned, he caught only the unmistakable white tale of a deer bounding into the trees.

"Hey, you can stay," he called after it. "As long as you don't have a camera."

The deer kept running, clearly unimpressed by Jason's concession.

Jason rested his hip against the railing and searched in vain for more wildlife. Sydney had mentioned deer, caribou, bighorn sheep, and lemmings, although Jason wouldn't know a lemming if it popped up and said hello. She'd also mentioned foxes, wolves, wolverines, and grizzlies, although she'd assured him those were more elusive. Jason had jokingly told her he'd rather face a grizzly than a photographer. Now, staring out into the woods that surrounded him, he wasn't so sure.

His eyes fell at last on the garage. It'd been built in the style of an old barn, with a tall, rounded roof. The big doors meant for cars were on the far side of the building. On the near side, there was only a single, person-sized doorway, with a cobblestone path leading to the mudroom off the kitchen. Jason eyed the window on the second floor. Had he really seen somebody in it?

He left his coffee cup on the porch and descended the front steps, angling off the path toward the garage, the frosty grass crunching under his bare feet. It was colder than he expected, each step worse than the one before, and he ended up doing an ungraceful skip-hop-hop across the frozen ground, trying to walk without letting his feet touch the ground any longer than necessary. He imagined he looked like those idiots who walked across coals, so he stopped when he reached the cobblestones and glanced around, hoping no photographers had shown up to capture it on film. No matter how innocuous the activity, the tabloids always managed to put a tantalizing spin on things. He imagined the headlines.

Jadon Walker Buttermore on Drugs! Thinks the Ground Is Hot Lava!

JayWalk in the Throes of Drug-Induced Hallucination!

JayWalking His Way to the Loony Bin!

Not as sensational as a sex tape, but still enough to sell a few copies.

His paranoia proved unwarranted. He saw no sign of trespassers. Then again, he hadn't seen the photographer who'd taken the pictures of him and Dylan eight months earlier, either. He hadn't known until Natalie called him the next morning that he'd made *StarWatch*'s cover once again. In some ways, it had been a relief. He'd been debating the best way to come out for ages. But being outed in such a sensational way hadn't been part of the plan.

He glanced toward his bedroom, and the second-floor porch, where he and Dylan had made out the night before. He shuddered, thinking how careless he'd been. Some people said there was no such thing as bad press, but those people had clearly never been caught in a tabloid's crosshairs.

"Can't let that happen again," he mumbled as he turned toward the garage.

The door was nothing special. A four-paned window up top, solid wood below. He tried the knob, but found it locked. Nothing of interest when he peered inside, either. Empty spaces where cars belonged and empty shelves along the walls. He knew from viewing the floor plans that the staircase to the guesthouse lay directly to his right, along the same interior wall that held the door, but he couldn't see it.

He tried the knob a second time, for no good reason whatsoever. Still locked. Not that he'd expected that to change.

If a photographer had found their way inside, would they have thought to lock the door behind them? Would they still be up there, or had they snuck out during the night?

Jason crouched and inspected the cobblestones at his feet, searching for footprints, or—

Well, to be honest, he didn't know what exactly. Maybe a note written in chalk, "The paparazzi was here"?

He found nothing but dirt and damp cobblestones.

He crossed back over to the house, confident that he looked less ridiculous than he had the first time. He went quietly up the stairs, wondering if Dylan was still asleep. He imagined crawling under his new down comforter, snuggling into the familiar warmth of Dylan's arms, maybe making love one more time before saying good-bye. It disappointed him to find Dylan already up and half-dressed.

"Hey, there you are," Dylan said as he buttoned his shirt. His jeans were on too, although his feet were still bare.

Jason settled on the bed and crossed his legs. "Are you leaving already?"

"I have a flight to catch."

"I see." Jason had driven his car full of belongings to Idaho and checked into a motel in nearby Coeur d'Alene a few days before the closing. He'd been thrilled when Dylan had called at the last minute and told him he'd booked a flight to Spokane and would be there in time to help Jason with the move. And now here they were: Jason's bags still sitting in his car in the driveway, and Dylan already with one foot out the door.

Jason fiddled with the ragged hem of his jeans, debating. He wanted to ask what was so urgent that Dylan had to rush out before breakfast. He wanted to suggest that Dylan stay, if not another night, at least a few more hours. But he couldn't figure out how to say any of it without sounding desperate.

"I have an appointment for new head shots at four," Dylan went on. "And then later tonight . . ." He grinned mischievously. "I have a hot date."

Jason's heart sank. "Oh?"

"Remember Tryss?"

"Victim Number Five, from *Summer Camp Nightmare 3*?"

"That's the one. Poor girl has daddy issues from here to the moon, a failed acting career, and a boob job she's still paying off. It's like the desperation trifecta." He winked. "Even you couldn't turn that down."

"I *have* turned that down."

Dylan laughed and perched on the edge of the love seat to pull on his shoes. When he glanced up again, Jason was surprised to find his expression somber. "It was good seeing you, Jase."

Jason did his best to keep his tone casual when he answered. "You too."

"I had a great time last night."

"So did I." But those words didn't sound casual at all. Jason knew his heartache had crept into his voice, but Dylan showed no sign of having heard it as he crossed the room and put a hand on either side of Jason's face, leaning close to peer into his eyes.

"You know I love you, right?"

Jason's heart leapt. He swallowed hard. "You do?"

"Of course. You're like a brother to me. You know that."

Jason was pretty sure most brothers didn't do what they'd done the night before, but he didn't argue. He only hoped Dylan couldn't see how much those words hurt him. "I love you too." He was proud that he managed to keep his voice steady.

And casual.

"You'll call me if you need anything, right?" Dylan asked.

Jason nodded. "Right," he lied.

"Good." Dylan kissed him—not like a brother, certainly, but not quite like a lover either.

Like a friend.

"Take care, JayWalk."

"You too."

And then Dylan walked down the stairs. Out the front door. Jason refused to watch. He only listened as Dylan's car crunched over the gravel drive toward the main road.

And then there was only Jason, and the solitude he'd longed for so desperately.

Funny how solitude and loneliness felt so much alike.